REAPER

KRIS MICHAELS

WWW.KRISMICHAELSAUTHOR.COM

CHAPTER 1

S *even Days Ago*:

Sometimes, in Reaper's profession, road-blocks happened. This one required a bulldozer to move. Good thing that he specialized in bulldozer tactics. His target, a paranoid son of a bitch, had good reason to worry. The man had the blood of thousands on his hands. His country's death toll, based on his orders, captured the attention of the Council. The multinational organization that included Guardian Security cleansed scum like this bastard from the Earth. The man inside that mansion had been coded for assassination by the Council. His target's lust for the blood of his coun-trymen would end tonight. It was Reaper's mission to ensure it did.

Disabling the antiquated alarm system in this third-world country was as simple as looping the system back onto itself. Reaper had performed the task so many times, he could do it in his sleep. The locks on the side entrance were sturdy, and it took him a grand total of thirty seconds to defeat the deadbolt. He slipped into the garage and locked the door behind him. The guards that wandered the property did periodic checks on locked doors. His surveillance of his objective had been thorough, albeit rushed. His target changed plans often; again, the man's paranoia played out in predictable unpredictability.

Reaper had enough information to complete his assignment. The roadblocks... well, he'd deal with them as they came. From his count, there were three guards on duty tonight inside the villa. The count hadn't been verified, and because of his target's travel plans tomorrow, Reaper had to act tonight.

He made his way to the three doors that led into the villa from the garage. One went to the servants' quarters, where the off-duty guards were berthed. The second led into the kitchen and the third a hallway leading to the foyer. He opened the door that led into the hallway. The lights were out and his black clothing and felt-soled shoes made him a silent ghost along the wall.

He made it to the foyer and sprinted up the stairs to his right. At the top of the stairs, he slipped into the first door. Silently, he moved through the small bedroom and exited through the window. He lifted himself up and out onto a decorative ledge that ran above the second-floor windows. His size and bulk made the balance beam effort difficult but not impossible. With a side shuffle, his back pinned to the stucco, he moved to the corner of the house.

With a quick glance, Reaper confirmed the balcony was empty. He rounded the corner and dropped onto the travertine tiles soundlessly. A cough from inside stilled his movements. He backed into the corner of the second-floor patio and waited. Two of his target's guards walked out onto the patio. One leaned against the rail and withdrew a package of cigarettes. The other fished out a lighter. Reaper watched and waited. They both turned to look out at the night. He launched.

Three steps later, he grabbed the nearest guard's chin and the back of his head, snapping his neck. The other guard, momentarily surprised, froze for a split second. It was all the time Reaper needed. He extended his arm and sliced through the muscle of the guard's throat. It wasn't a clean cut, but it was deep enough.

The gurgled, surprised release of air wasn't very loud, but it was loud enough. A third guard spoke from his post inside. Reaper dipped back into the darkness, leaving the bodies in sight. The inside guard spoke again, frustrated this time. Sliding along the rail, Reaper inched up to the door.

When the third guard appeared, Reaper struck out with his knife. The guard shifted just enough that the knife attack wasn't fatal. The man's hand went for his holstered weapon. Reaper flew into action. Close quarters fighting was his specialty. He struck down the man's hand, shoved his knife into the guard's gut, and strong armed the razor-sharp edge of the weapon up toward the man's heart, ripping open his abdominal cavity. Natural reaction folded the man on himself. Reaper turned, grabbed the guard's hair, lifted his head, and applied enough pressure to cut the man's carotid artery and windpipe. The snap of cartilage and sinewed muscles was indication of how deep he'd cut.

He dropped his grip on the man's head and let the body drop. With practiced ease, he dipped down and wiped the blood from his weapon on the body's clothes. Reaper heard the soft footsteps behind him and reacted. He twisted and thrust up with the knife at the same time a fourth man struck down with his knife. The damn thing hit home above his hip. Reaper jerked his knife up, gutting the man above him in the same way he'd killed the other guard.

Pitching to move out of the way of the dead man's fall, he rolled and popped up into his fighting stance. He waited, listening intently. Nothing except the sound of dead and dying bodies contracting, the muscles twitching and gasses escaping.

Death was ugly, but he knew it well.

Reaper lifted and made his way to the suite where his target waited. He opened the door and slipped into the room. A paunchy, middle-aged man looked up from his desk. Reaper strode toward him as the man freaked and grappled for the drawer that undoubtedly held a gun. He lifted his knife and let it fly. The blade's strike didn't kill the target, but it gave Reaper the time he needed. His target fell from his desk chair and started crawling away.

Reaper caught up with the man and planted his foot on his back, forcing him to the ground. Spittle flew from the man's mouth as he raged, "I'll kill everyone you've ever loved. I'll kill everyone you've ever known. My guards will be here before you can kill me."

Reaper flipped a small latch on his belt buckle and pulled. His garrote slid from where it was hidden. He bent down and wrapped it around the man's neck, using it to force the man to his feet. Reaper moved him back to his chair at his desk.

His target wheezed, "I'll pay you triple, four times what they are paying you. You'll never have to work again."

Reaper leaned down and whispered, "I love what I do. I'm death's messenger. I am the Reaper and your time on earth is over. Hell is your next stop." He lifted away and crossed the wire garrote behind the man's neck. With all the strength he possessed, he pulled. The thin, sharp wire severed muscle, tendon, and bone. His target's head fell forward and rolled onto his desk.

Reaper wrapped his garrote around his wrist, retrieved his knife, and walked out of the office. He made it to the patio before he noticed his blood-soaked shirt. The wound didn't matter. After a glance to make sure there was no one making a walk-through of the grounds below, he dropped over the railing, back into the shadows where he existed.

. . .

Present-day:

Reaper parked on an inroad of the darkened, woody foothills of upper Pennsylvania. The smell of home hit him as he tried to unfold from the midsize SUV he'd rented. Holding onto the door, he straightened as far as he could without opening the knife wound that was festering and feverish.

The mix of birch, maple, and ash trees he'd pulled into presented a musty smell of leaf decomposition that lingered in between gentle breezes of mountain air. He was home, or at least, he was back to where he'd grown up. Lake Garden, Pennsylvania, boasted about four hundred people and had changed little since he'd left the town.

His interest didn't lay in the town or the wooded foothills where he'd parked. No, what he wanted to see was further along the trail. He followed a ghost of an old path through the trees, using the long, tall saplings that had filled in the old trail as support. He stopped short of exposing himself and stared across a plowed field. He blinked and wiped at his eyes. This was all wrong. Instead of the small farmhouse, a large, modern house now dominated the landscape. The old sheds were gone, the barn painted, and new paddocks held beautiful horses and foals.

Reaper leaned back against a tree. A truck rambled down the dirt road to the house. A man and two children got out. An acid-tipped spear of dread lanced his gut, dulling the pain from his actual wound. He moved slightly so he could see the front of the house. A tall, dark-haired woman exited and scooped up the smallest child. The other ran into the house as the man mounted the steps and kissed the woman.

Sagging with relief, he rested against the birch tree that was supporting the majority of his weight. That wasn't Harmony. He stared at the mini-mansion standing where the small farmhouse had once stood. *Where was she?* He shoved his weight forward and ping-ponged off trees as he made his way back to the SUV. He wasn't a welcomed visitor in this town, but there was one place he could go for the information he needed.

He folded into the vehicle again and dropped his head against the steering wheel. His breath was ragged and the fever he'd been ignoring was starting to kick his ass. He started the car and backed out of the woods.

Six miles later, he pulled up in front of a building

he knew well. The shingle on the door still hung there. Maggie Cooper, M.D. He pulled himself out of the SUV and made his way to the door. He lifted a hand to knock, but the door opened.

She hadn't changed much. Her silver hair was a little longer, but there was fire in her eyes and a healthy look around her. "Roman Alexander. I thought you'd be dead by now."

He winced and propped an arm against the door frame. "Not yet, Maggie." He lifted his shirt, exposing his festering wound. "Although if you don't help me, today might be the day."

The door opened farther, and Maggie backed up. "You know the way."

He did. Reaper pushed off the door frame and shuffled into the exam room which was once the formal dining room but had served as Maggie's clinic for as long as he could remember.

"Lay back and jack that shirt up." She pulled the doors closed behind them. "What happened?"

"Bad day at the office about a week back." He grimaced and swallowed hard when he twisted to lay down.

Maggie whipped her hair into a ponytail and then snapped on a pair of gloves. "Knife?"

He nodded. "Didn't move fast enough."

"This is bad. If you'd waited any longer, you'd have to be transported to one of the big hospitals." She grabbed an IV stand and set it beside the hospital bed he was laying on. She turned back to gather more supplies. When she returned, she inserted the IV port and hooked him up to it. "Going to give you something for the infection and work on hydrating you."

"Hydrating?"

She pinched his skin. "When your skin doesn't bounce back into place like this, you need fluids. I'm going to have to clean this mess out to see what I'm expected to fix. It isn't going to be pleasant."

"Do what you have to do, Mags." He closed his eyes and found that spot somewhere between consciousness and darkness where he and Harmony lived a happy life on that little farm.

He woke with a start. Maggie was sitting beside him with a huge cup of something that steamed. He watched the whiffs of heat rise off it for a moment. "You knocked me out."

"I did what I had to do. Isn't that what you told me to do? Now, for my sanity, please, lie to me and tell me that you're on the right side of the law." Maggie took a sip from her mug.

"I don't have to lie, Mags. I work for a security company." *As an assassin.* That piece of information didn't need to be released, however.

The woman lowered her cup and stared at him. "They don't have insurance or doctors?"

He chuffed out a lungful of air. "They do. I chose not to use them."

"Ah, that death wish you had as a child still has a hold of you?" Maggie took another sip.

He blinked at her. "What?"

"Come on, Roman. Why else would you have done half the shit you did? And don't tell me you didn't kill Bert Graham before you left because I wouldn't believe it for a second." Maggie leaned back in her chair and crossed her legs, defying him to deny what he'd done.

"If I had killed him, I'd be in prison, not working for one of the largest security companies in the world." He shifted and winced. The wound had been covered with a patch of white gauze. "What's the verdict on the hole in my side?"

"The verdict is you've got an angel sitting on your shoulder. Nothing of much importance damaged. I stitched you up and I'm pumping you full of antibiotics. You'll need to keep your ass in that bed for another twenty-four hours. If you think about moving, I won't tell you where Harmony went." His head snapped in Maggie's direction. "See, this old woman isn't as stupid or as blind as you young folk think I am. What the hell were you thinking, leaving that girl? She loved you, you big, stupid lug."

Reaper blinked at Maggie. He knew her well; she was best friends with Tom Rada, the man who had taken him in after his father had died. The man he called uncle and the only family he had. Yes, he'd avenged his uncle by killing that bastard Bert Graham. No one else knew the truth. No one except Harmony. Killing Bert had brought Demos into his life, yet all of that history wasn't important. He pinned Maggie with a laser-focused stare. "I was no good for her."

"Well, no kidding, but you were all she's ever seen. She never looked at another man, just kept looking down that gravel road for you to come back."

He hated that the information made him happy. She *should* have found someone else. She *should* have a full life with a family and her art, and yet, he took a perverse pleasure in the fact that she longed for him as much as he longed for her. "Where did she go?"

Maggie smiled at him. "I'll tell you everything when I unhook you from that IV. Not a second before. Now, I've got some soup heating up. Let's crank that bed up a bit and get something warm inside you. I'll bring you up to speed on all the gossip while you eat." She set her cup down and took her time rising from the chair. It was then he noticed how age had settled into her joints and the lines of her face had grown deeper.

"I can't stay, Maggie." He needed his phone. He may have already missed a check-in.

"Don't argue with me." She pointed a finger at him. "You're staying right here. I moved your fancy little crossover thingy to the old barn and brought in your phone and bag." His eyes flitted to the corner of the room where she pointed. "No, I didn't go through your bag. I thought for sure you were running from the law."

He smiled for the first time. "No, ma'am, but I do need to check-in. May I have my phone, please?"

Maggie crossed the room and came back with his phone. "I'll go get that soup so you can talk in private." She shuffled out of the room and drew the door closed behind her.

Reaper waited until he couldn't hear her any longer before he called in.

"Operator Two-Seven-Four, stand by, Sunset Operative Fourteen."

"Affirmative." He closed his eyes and waited for Anubis to come online.

"You missed a check-in. Authenticate Shallow."

"Grave. I missed a check-in because an injury I sustained on the last mission became infected and I needed to treat it."

"That would have been something to put into your out-brief on your last mission." Anubis' growled reprimand made it through the airwaves loud and clear.

"It wasn't that bad, and I thought it was healing. I made it through my video Go/No Go with flying colors."

"From now on, you'll make a notification if you break a fingernail, or you'll be back at the Rose running the course until Hell freezes over or Fury forgives you. Understood?"

"Completely. It won't happen again." Damn, Hell had a better chance of freezing over than Fury forgiving him for a fuck up like not reporting an injury.

"How long will it keep you out?"

"A week. No longer." He wouldn't let that happen.

"Check in with me tomorrow at the correct time.

You have a mission. I'll give you the details after I confirm the delay won't cause any issues." There was no room for argument in Anubis' directive

"Roger that."

"Annex out."

He dropped his head back on the pillow. Fuck, he should have reported the injury or at the least told Smoke he was hurt and gotten help from the Guardian docs, but instead, he had to come north.

He had to see her.

Not that he'd ever contact her. He watched her from the trees like a pathetic loser. She needed to move on, and by the looks of the small farm, she had. He'd bide his time here until Maggie told him where she'd gone. Maybe then he'd be able to close this chapter of his life. God knows he couldn't prevent himself from coming back here. With her gone, he'd be able to walk away.

Maggie opened the door and wheeled in a small cart with two large bowls of soup, half a loaf of homemade bread, and a plate of butter. "I figured we could talk while we ate. I don't get much company anymore. They put up one of those community health centers in town. Medical residents rotate through and see people for free. I can't compete with those rates." She moved to the side of his bed and used the hand crank to elevate him to a reclined sitting position. She rolled a steel tray that went over the bed and put his bowl, silverware, and a slice of thickly buttered bread on the tray before serving herself, using the cart as her table.

He took a bite of her homemade chicken vegetable soup; the homemade taste of stewed chicken woke his hunger. "Delicious. Thank you."

She waved a hand. "You don't look like you've missed too many meals. You were always a big kid, but it looks like you've been working out."

He chuckled. "It's required in my profession." Keeping himself in top physical condition was automatic. Well, until the knife wound.

"Figured. Where do you work for this security firm?"

"Overseas."

"Huh." Maggie tore off a piece of bread and ate it before she spoke again. "Ever in France?"

"On and off. Why? You want me to send you some perfume?" He held his spoon halfway to his mouth as he waited for her to speak.

The old woman hooted with laughter. "No, thanks, but I can think of a million other things I'd want before I'd want perfume."

"Then why the curiosity?"

She pointed at the IV. "Nothing more till that comes out."

"Is Harmony's cousin dead?"

Maggie looked up from her meal. She nodded once and finished what was in her mouth. "Delbert picked on the wrong man. The drunk son of a bitch actually started the fight. The guy told him to back off, warned him not to punch him again. Delbert put him on the ground and tried to choke him when he was down. The guy shook him off, did some kind of martial arts move—one of them flying kicks straight to ole Del's head. Snapped his neck clean as a whistle between the C1 and C2 vertebrae."

Reaper ate another spoonful of the rich soup before he spoke, "Still the county's coroner, I assume."

"It pays the bills. It also lets me know what's going on. Like when Bert Graham died. Beat to a pulp. Someone took out a lot of rage on that man. That type of rage is rare. I have no doubt that would have left some miserable bruising on the perp's fists. Kind of like the bruising you had the next day when I saw you hitchhiking south."

"There was nothing left for me here with Tom dead."

"That girl was here, you idiot."

"Again, I was no good for her."

"Boy, I'm not arguing that fact. Just don't say there was nothing here for you. It isn't true."

Reaper ate a couple more spoonfuls of soup before he asked, "Did Bert's family ever sell that land?"

"Nope. Everything is sitting there rotting to the ground. I drive by every now and again to say hello to Tom. I keep his gravestone cleared. Funny how that thing just showed up. Fancy marker, too. Must have been heavy to set up in the middle of the night."

Reaper leveled a stare at the doctor. There was nothing in his expression. He'd learned how to hide every trace of emotion. "I wouldn't know."

Maggie narrowed her eyes at him and held his glare for several long seconds before she dropped her eyes. "The world has hardened you, Roman. You were a rambunctious one, always getting into fights, but you're different now."

"Life has hardened me, Maggie."

"Perhaps that's for the best. You need to stay away from here. Bert's family still swears it was you that killed him. If you're here, they'll start kicking up dust again. Besides, there really is nothing here for you now. Especially since Harmony sold the land and left."

Reaper finished his bowl of soup and a second piece of bread before he asked, "How long has Harmony been in Paris?"

Maggie's eyes flicked up to him. "I didn't *say* she was in Paris."

"You didn't have to; she wanted to live and paint in Paris for as long as I can remember. She used to draw the pictures she saw in the encyclopedia Delbert's folks kept at the house. She painted them, too, when she could scrape together the money for supplies. She was damn good. The Impressionist era was her passion if I recall correctly."

He'd arranged for paint supplies to be delivered anonymously to the house every now and again, always on Friday nights when Delbert would be out drinking. Hopefully, Harmony was able to paint while she lived with him. If the bastard found the supplies or her art, he'd sell them both for booze money. It was a risk he hoped she'd taken.

"She'd been in communication with someone over there. Delbert had sold one of the paintings she made. A copy of one of those water lily pictures, a Monet, I believe. There was a big splash about them trying to sell counterfeit paintings, you know? But she signed her name on the paintings. She wasn't doing anything but practicing. Delbert got into a slew of trouble and got a warning from the state police and the FBI. That was the talk of the town for a long time, let me tell you."

"You said she'd talked to someone in Paris?"

"Yup, an art professor at one of those private schools. Said he found out about her through a contest she entered."

"She entered a contest?" That didn't sound like the Harmony he knew.

Maggie set her spoon down. "See, that's the thing. She didn't remember entering a contest, but this guy was legit. She did her research on the school and such. She had to turn him down. Didn't have the money to go over there and live even though he offered her a scholarship to pay for the lessons, but after Delbert got himself killed, it took her the snap of a finger to sell the land and leave."

He pushed the silver tray away as he processed the information. "I hope she's happy."

"She's away from here, which was a good thing. You and Harmony never stood a chance here, you know. You were both eagles in a cage."

He lifted his eyes and looked at her. "Explain that, please?"

She chortled. "Eagles mate for life and need a

grand vista to fly. You'd have both withered and died in this little speck of a town."

"How long has she been gone?"

"Nine months or so." Maggie stood and placed his dishes on the little cart. She cranked the bed back down so he was reclined a bit more. "Bathroom location hasn't changed. Take that bag with you if you need to go. There is a hook on the wall next to the toilet. Use it. If you leave before I wake up, I'll take payment in cash. You have enough of it in your wallet."

Roman smiled as the old woman left the room and closed the door behind her. She was a fixture in Lake Garden and knew a hell of a lot more than she'd ever let anyone know. She'd patched him up from adolescence to young adulthood. Broken bones, cuts, concussions, it had always been Maggie that his uncle had brought him to.

He closed his eyes and drew a deep breath. She was a part of his past. And this would be the last conversation they'd ever have.

CHAPTER 2

Harmony glanced from her canvas to the picture beside her. This month, she was learning the brush stroke and technique of Auguste Renoir. The light bar she was using kept the exact lighting she needed regardless of the time of day. There were no windows in her studio, nothing to distract her from her lessons. Even though impressionists focused on the utilization of shadow and light in direct contradiction to the perfectionist modeling in the renaissance era, she couldn't afford to deviate from the standard she was required to achieve. So, she didn't add or detract from the master's work. The quick, seemingly spontaneous brushstrokes were meant to look loose and as if they were capturing the light of the scene and not the scene itself. She meticulously recreated each famous painting after weeks of learning the swoop and curve the artist used. Natural long and short flat hog hair paintbrushes, cut and angled specifically to match the width and depth of drag, took days to trim just right. But she was on a scholarship; perfection was mandatory if she wanted to continue to learn from some of the best minds in the industry.

She examined the stroke on her canvas and the corresponding stroke on the 3-D photograph. She could see a minor imperfection in her stroke, but this project was due to her professor in two weeks. Starting over wasn't an option. It was, however, time to stop for the day. Her eyes felt the strain of studying the painting and her back and arm needed a break. Holding the brushes in a contrived grip to enable her to duplicate the stroke exactly without shaking was harder than most would assume.

She dipped her brushes into mineral oil and cleaned them before she turned off the light in her studio and opened the door. She stopped halfway into her living room. "Talib, what are you doing here?"

Talib Behar crossed his legs and looked at her. The scrape of his gaze over her body made her feel naked even though she was completely covered. "You left your door unlocked."

She glanced at the door and then back at him. She'd hadn't, she remembered checking it before she'd gone into her studio this morning, but how could she dispute the fact the man was sitting on her small couch?

"We will be going to Cannes in a fortnight. There is an exhibit I want you to see. I expect you to have eveningwear and be presentable."

She blinked at the outright command. Since she'd arrived, Talib had become more and more demanding. Her primary instructor, Bernard LaVette, had introduced them the day she'd moved into the apartment she leased. She lived on a tight budget and her saved money was dwindling quickly even if she didn't have to pay for the lessons she was receiving. "I don't have money to spend on gowns. I can barely afford to pay rent and eat." Rent in Paris, especially close to the city center, was outrageous, but this was where she was required to live to receive the scholarship for her tuition.

Talib stood. He was handsome; his parents were Saudi nationals who'd moved to Monaco before he was born. She'd researched him after the first time he assumed liberties with her. His mother died years ago, and his father was the owner of the crown jewel of casinos that dotted the small country. Talib Behar was filthy rich, and his mannerisms and impeccable taste in clothes, cars, and expensive jewelry spoke to that fact with an ease that could only be matured from birth.

"I have repeatedly told you that I will pay for this hovel and anything else you need." He moved to her and grabbed her ponytail. "A trip to the spa for hair and skin would not be amiss."

"No." She pulled her hair from his hand and walked the six steps to her small kitchen area. She had a tiny refrigerator, a hot plate, a toaster, and a sink which was barely adequate but functional.

He laughed, and it wasn't a pleasant sound. She'd had this conversation one too many times. Talib wanted her to repay him with sex. She wasn't going there. The man's slender good looks and almost effeminate mannerisms weren't her cup of tea.

"Bella, you can't keep putting me off." Talib moved up behind her and trapped her at the sink as she washed her hands.

"I can and I will. I won't be forced into a sexual relationship with anyone." She didn't look back at him and hated the way his hips pinned her. His interest was more than evident.

"The trip to Cannes is required. Your dear Bernard should have mentioned it by now. I'll make sure he remembers what he promised." He pulled the band out of her sandy blonde hair and it fell in waves over her shoulders.

She turned off the water and reached for a towel. In doing so, she leaned forward. Talib pushed harder, bending her over the lip of the sink. She froze. It was the most aggressive he'd ever been. She spat the words at him, "Get away from me, Talib, or you'll see how I protect myself. You'll be singing soprano for a year."

He leaned forward and whispered, "Vulgar American. I love that about you, Bella. I bet you're a hellcat."

"You'll never find out," she ground out through her teeth.

"Oh, I will."

She shoved him away with an elbow to his gut. "Don't think this is foreplay. It isn't. I was raised country hard, Talib, and if you don't know what that means, then look it up. I'm not someone you can push into a corner with threats. I'm immune to your verbal bullshit."

The man leaned back against her. "I will tame your fire, little one. LaVette will be here tomorrow.

Ask him *why* you'll do as I ask. I expect you to be ready and wear the clothes I will purchase and have delivered. You *will* go to Cannes. I *will* pay for everything, and you *will* pay me back." He swiveled his hips.

If she didn't think decking the bastard would get her expelled, she'd have whipped her head back and broken his nose. Instead, she looked over her shoulder at him. "I will not accept the clothes, nor will I go to Cannes with you. I'll leave Paris first. Take a hint."

"Oh, my dear, hissing kitten, you won't leave Paris. It is not in the cards." He stepped away from her and sauntered out of her apartment, leaving the door open in his wake. She stalked over to the door and closed it quietly. An eerie sense of foreboding crawled over her skin, leaving a slithering worry buried deep inside. She ran her hands through her hair and fell back against the door, sliding to her butt.

Harmony stared out the window at the building across the street. The white plaster fascia was crumbling under the window. The decay mirrored her dreams. She'd hoped to be able to explore her talent, but according to the class schedule, the first two years of formal training were to be spent learning the masters. It made sense. In a way. She did long for interaction with the other students, but the professors came to her apartment; she never went to the campus that she'd seen on the website. It was due to a complete rehab of the campus, or so she was told.

Her nerves were shot. Talib's unwanted appearance had thrown her out of whack. She pulled out her phone and did the math. She opened the app and called Maggie, the only person in Lake Garden with whom she kept in contact.

"I was just thinking about you. How's Paris?" Maggie's familiar voice washed over her like a shower of spring rain, refreshing and lifegiving.

"I'm doing okay. How's things in Lake Garden? Any good gossip?"

"Well, let's see. Madge Randall finally kicked Seth out. He went out, got drunk, and then went back home, broke down the front door, and put her in the hospital. The sheriff and his deputy rounded up Seth, who allegedly had no recollection of what happened. Judge Taylor gave him the max and told him maybe he'd remember if he had time to think. Both the judge and the sheriff had been after Madge to tell the truth about her injuries for years. You know they don't tolerate a man who beats on a woman."

She'd graduated high school with Madge. The girl was the head cheerleader, and her husband Seth was the starting quarterback. Only after they were married did the entire town figure out that Seth was better at using his fists than the wrenches at the machine shop where he worked. "Is Madge going to be okay?"

"She's filed for divorce, packed up, and moved away, so I guess so." Maggie sighed. "Something's been eating me for a while now. Roman stopped by."

She closed her eyes and dropped her head back against the door, gutted. "He came home? Why? When?" *Had she missed him coming back to get her?*

"No, he wasn't coming home. He just stopped by. It was just over three months ago. He hasn't changed, honey."

"He has to have changed; it's been ten years," she half-laughed the rebuttal.

"Well, true. He's bigger, a lot more muscle, and as handsome as always, but I could tell he was still a troublemaker."

"How's that?"

"He gave me a line about working for a company. Overseas. Asked about you and figured out you moved to Paris."

Her eyes popped open. "What did you tell him?"

Maggie made an irritated noise. "That you had an opportunity and you took it. Which is true. Paris is huge, he couldn't find you. Unless you wanted to see him?"

"No, that relationship is long gone." Not of their choosing, but life had a way of breaking up things that weren't meant to be.

"Figured, that's why I didn't give him your new number. How's classes going?"

She sighed, "I'm learning. I'm feeling confident in my abilities and my projects have kept me in the scholarship, so good, I guess."

"Ah, yeah, I recognize that tone. You used it when Delbert was being an ass and you didn't want to complain about it, but you needed to talk."

"It's just Talib. He's... persistent."

"Grab his balls and squeeze as hard as you can, that will make him back off you." Maggie's razor-sharp response cut through the connection.

She barked a laugh. "It might come to that. Anyway, he was saying that there is an exhibit at Cannes I needed to attend. Maggie, I don't have the money for the clothes, the hotel, or the food. If I don't deviate from my budget an iota, I have just enough to finish school and fly home." Although she had nowhere to stay once she got back to the states, but she'd worry about that problem when she got to it. "I kind of miss painting the mountains." She'd earned some pretty good money selling a couple of her paintings in Felder's Whistle Stop Shop, which was basically a tourist shop for those people wandering through the Adirondacks. Then Delbert sold one of her copies of the masters' work and all hell had busted loose. She'd been terrified when the FBI knocked on their door that night.

"You stand your ground, and that professor of yours should be discouraging Talib from being an ass. You need to bring it up to him and tell him you're not happy." Maggie's statement was true, but damn it, she really didn't want to rock the boat. Her skills had grown a hundred-fold since she'd been in Paris. Just the ability to paint all day was a dream come true but receiving one-on-one instruction— that was something she wasn't willing to jeopardize.

"I really don't want to cause any issues, Maggie."

"You'd rather crawl between the sheets with that man?"

She stared at the paint under her fingernails. *Would it be that bad?* Her track record at picking out a good man wasn't exactly encouraging. She'd picked Roman and look where that got her. No, she couldn't blame him. He had nothing in Lake Garden after his uncle was killed. They found Bert's body two days after he disappeared. Everyone knew he'd retaliated and killed Bert, but no one could prove it. The 'hunting accident' Bert had concocted was a load of cow dung. Bert shot Tom in the back. They weren't friends and didn't hunt together. But Bert had the old sheriff in his back pocket, and that was another reason Roman had to get out of town.

"You still there?"

Maggie's question roused her from her musings. "I am. I'm probably making more out of this than necessary. I've been pushing myself hard lately. I'm tired."

"Go out and get a bottle of wine and some of that fancy cheese, slap it on a baguette, and get yourself toasted. A good drunk every now and again never hurt anyone."

Harmony laughed although her heart wasn't in it. With an apparently unlockable lock on her door, she wasn't going to let herself become impaired, but Maggie didn't need to know that. "That sounds like a plan. Thanks for the gossip. I'll call you again soon."

"Take care of yourself, girl. Don't let that bastard have what he wants. Come back home if you need to. You know you can stay here with me until you get your feet under you."

She smiled and closed her eyes. "Oh, Maggie, thank you for the offer, but I'll be fine. I'll call soon. Bye."

She waited until Maggie hung up before she let the first tear fall. What was she going to do if Talib pressed the issue? Was the trip to Cannes required? There was no way it could be. She hadn't seen it on the website when she looked up the instruction modules. "Stop it. You've made it through worse," she spoke out loud, trying to snap herself out of her anxiety. She *had* gone through a lot in her twenty-eight years.

Talib was a tiny blip on the screen that was filled with jagged mountains, the biggest of which was Roman. God, how she'd loved that man. He was two years older than her, and they'd been inseparable since he'd moved in with Tom Rada who lived next door to her aunt and uncle.

They were both without parents. Her mom died in childbirth and her father had dropped her off with his sister to raise when she was two years old. She'd seen her father a grand total of three times after that.

Delbert was her aunt's son, and the boy had hated her for as long as she could remember. When Roman found Delbert hitting her with a switch in the forest between the two farms, he'd pushed Delbert down and stood in front of her. Roman had a deep voice even as an adolescent. He pointed at Delbert and snarled, "You touch her again and I will whoop the hell out of you."

Delbert still verbally abused her, but he never lifted a hand against her even after Roman left. She often wondered what Roman had done to keep Delbert in line. God, she missed Roman. He was her best friend, her first lover, and the love of her life.

Looking around the small apartment, she shook her head. She'd give all of this up—the lessons, living in Paris, and learning from people who had perfected Impressionist techniques—to have him back. She shook her head and pulled her butt off the floor. There was no need to sit there and daydream about what would never happen. She needed to eat and then she'd lose herself in a book. That part of her life was over. Roman had left her and Lake Garden.

For him, there was no other choice.

CHAPTER 3

R eaper closed the file on his secure computer. He powered down the laptop and secured it in his Italian leather slimline briefcase. Standing, he made his way over to the windows and stared out at the sidewalk that ran along Croisette Beach. It was already overflowing with people. He glanced at his watch. According to the research he'd been given, his target was on one of the yachts that would anchor today.

He turned away from the window and sat back down, poured himself a cup of coffee that he'd ordered from room service, and mentally detailed his assignment. Chevalier Ardan, a billionaire businessman, had been coded. Reaper took a sip of his coffee and turned to look out the floor-to-ceiling windows.

Ardan had two faces. Publicly, he was a major sponsor of the arts. He was the main supporter of the film festival and was the premiere benefactor of the Louvre. His darker side, however, revealed the reason Reaper was in Cannes. Ardan and the consortium he was at the helm of sold weapons on the black market, and not your Saturday Night Specials, either. Ardan was smart; his weapons were ghost weapons, manufactured by hand with parts found readily available on the internet which now had no serial numbers. Outside the law? Yes. Worthy of being coded? No. At least, not until the weapons were used to kill a sitting president in a Caribbean Island massacre that shocked the world and instigated mass protests where seventeen more influential people in the president's political party were killed. Not 'assassinated' in the professional sense. He'd examined the pictures. Whatever entity had killed the party leaders had left evidence, and the first teams on the island, Guardian Assets, had found the link. A single cell phone was the match that flamed the tinder under Ardan's ass.

Guardian rarely bound his hands when it came to

the method or timing of his target's demise, but this time, they wanted the man shadowed. He snorted a laugh. Anubis assured him there was no pun intended. Right.

As the technicians for the CIA were tracing the phone calls from the phone found at the assassination site, two voice messages were dumped into voicemail. Apparently, whoever dropped the phone had failed to mention it to the higher-ups in his chain of command. The messages were vague, but if the extrapolations of the theorists with more brainpower than he'd ever had were correct, Ardan's consortium was meeting in Cannes. Tomorrow. Several other assets had been sprinkled around the city; he didn't know who, and he didn't care. When information on the players was discovered by Guardian operatives, his assignment would result in Ardan's final breath.

He sipped his coffee as his eyes flicked to the scantily clad beach goers stretched out on the powdered sugar-colored sands. A blonde in a red suit caught his eye. He stared at her for a moment. Taller than Harmony's five foot, five inches, by a half foot, it was a body he knew.

Valkyrie. He picked up the binoculars that were

sitting on his breakfast table and zoomed in on his fellow assassin. She turned heads as she walked down the beach toward the docks. He panned over and smiled. Ah, the yacht had arrived. Although Val was a deadly assassin, she was also one of the most beautiful women he'd ever seen. Her beauty could insinuate her into the tightest of circles. Obviously, Val was one of the operatives assigned to get information on Ardan.

He watched as the ship moored in the bay. It was far too big to fit into any of the berths that were constructed in the harbor. The helicopter on the back was overkill, but when you had as much money as Ardan, why not have a helicopter on your boat?

Reaper swung back to Val. She shook out a towel near the pier and lounged back in the sand, apparently oblivious to her surroundings. Looks were deceiving, to say the least. She'd gone through training with him, and she was good. She was finesse where he was brawn, but they'd worked together several times, using their opposite skills to wrap a net of death around a monster who preyed on those who couldn't protect themselves—demons like Ardan, who dealt in the world of death for profit.

Reaper put the binoculars down. Until he saw a transport ship from the yacht, watching was nothing more than a spectator sport. One he didn't feel inclined to play.

His phone vibrated on the white tablecloth.

"Target has arrived." Anubis' voice over the phone greeted him.

"I saw. Thirteen has a bird's-eye view."

There was a pause. "You have a visual?"

He chuckled. "Everyone has a visual. Her goal, I assume."

"Ah, her methods are unusual but effective."

"Very."

"We got the final sitrep on your last assignment. From the intel you picked up on the way out of the primary's office, we found four caves with over four hundred souls. Good work."

"Pure luck." He closed his eyes and thanked God he'd looked to his left and seen the small laptop.

"Training and experience. Consider this today's call-in. I'll call tomorrow."

"I'm ready." He'd reconned the expansive mansion that Ardan owned. It overlooked the city and had an impressive security system. Impressive but beatable. Guardian had the best thief in the world teaching them how to beat security systems. They had recurring training when new technology came to light. He leaned forward and stared at the super-yacht in the harbor, smiling to himself. Guardian went to extremes to hide the teacher's identity. They blacked out the screen and disguised his voice. Damn, he'd love to meet that man—or woman—and just listen to some of the jobs he or she'd done.

"Affirmative. Stand by for a green light. Reminder, it might not be tomorrow."

"I am aware." He acknowledged the fact if further intel was needed, his mission would be pushed back. On one hand, he hated the uncertainty; on the other, it was an adrenaline rush. He'd deal, no matter the timing.

"Annex out."

Reaper put his phone down on the table and took a sip of his tepid coffee. The bastard he'd been called away from Lake Garden to deal with lorded over the blood diamond trade with an iron fist, ruthlessly enslaving and killing thousands of his own people every year. The man rarely left his fortress but every year would fly to England to watch the two single's title matches at Wimbledon. Reaper was waiting for him in the makeshift office on his jet when the bastard flew home. He slit the man's throat, waited until they were in the right location, and then opened the cabin door and pulled his primary target out with him. By chance, he'd seen that small laptop and tucked it into his jump-suit while he waited. Once in the air, he let go of his target and pulled his ripcord. A high altitude high opening jump as his target catapulted to the ground. He'd never be identified. They told him the pilots were able to jump from the plane. He shrugged the information off. Align yourself with the devil and you get singed.

A movement near the yacht caught his eye. The smaller speed boat was being lowered. Time to go. He needed to identify his prey, see the man and his entourage.

Dressed in board shorts that weren't American and a plain black t-shirt, he made his way from his hotel to the pier, keeping his pace consistent but unhurried. He paused to read one of the historical markers along the way because Ardan was obviously getting his nails buffed before he boarded the trans-port boat. Once he noticed the smaller craft start toward the dock, he continued on his way. He jogged down the stairs by the pier and took a seat on the last stair, pulling his shoes off. That's when Ardan's advance team walked down the pier. Reaper crossed his leg and wiped the sand off his foot. He was fifty feet away from Val, but he'd never make contact in public. Ardan's men swept the pier and spoke into the comms they were wearing. Ardan leisurely sauntered out and...

Reaper hid the amusement he felt when Ardan did a double take in Valkyrie's direction. He stopped on the pier and leaned over the rail, directly above the beautiful, deadly assassin. He couldn't hear the conversation, but Val lifted up on her elbows; tipping her head back, she laughed. Ardan did too. So far, so good. Reaper brushed off his other foot and watched the men with his target. Hardened, battle tough. Good, that meant they were prior military, and even the best of men had habits learned or instilled by military training. They were punctual or early, never late. Attention to detail, focus on the job. Each of those traits was cataloged and filed in his head for future reference.

Valkyrie stood, still talking to Ardan. She flashed that beautiful smile at him, bent to pick up her towel, and then turned, walking away down the beach. If he was closer, he'd wager ten bucks Ardan had a string of drool dripping from his chin. The man watched Val for several minutes before he shook his head and started to walk toward the end of the pier.

Reaper put his shoes back on and walked up the stairs at the same time Ardan hit the sidewalk. A black sedan with darkened windows waited at the curb. Reaper glanced at the plate before he turned and walked the other direction. He repeated the plate letters and numbers to himself and sauntered back toward his room. There was no rush, and it was a beautiful day.

CHAPTER 4

Harmony answered the door, keeping the new chain she'd installed yesterday inserted in the locking mechanism. "Oh, hi. Just a minute." She shut the door, unlocked the chain, and opened it.

"What is this?" Bernard jiggled the chain.

"My door seems to have a broken lock. Talib let himself inside my apartment while I was working, even though I know I locked the door." The idea that Talib had managed to obtain a key to the apartment had started to take root because she'd tried the door numerous times from the outside and couldn't budge the locking mechanism without one.

"Ah, well, that would explain the chain." Bernard entered the house and made a straight line to the studio. "Show me what my favorite student has accomplished this week." He flicked on the studio light and headed straight for her easel. "Yes, yes. Very good. Exceptional." Bernard leaned over her work and then looked at the photograph. "The paint thickness is perfect and the strokes... magnificent. The color, however, is too dark." He stood up and glared at her.

"No, it isn't." She clicked on the light behind them and allowed him to re-examine the work.

"Ah, yes, this will be your best yet." He smiled and kept examining her brushstrokes.

"Thank you. Bernard, Talib said something about an exhibit in Cannes that I'll be required to attend." She watched his face fall as he straightened away from her painting.

"Come, we must take a picture so we can update the website first. I'll explain everything in due course."

She knew rushing Bernard was useless; he had a linear attention, focusing on what was important to him first. Then, if he felt like it, he'd address her concerns.

She stood with her paintbrushes beside the art she was copying. "I've never seen any of the pictures or videos you've done of me working on the website."

Bernard nodded. "Correct. Come let us talk." He turned and walked out of the studio. She returned her brushes to their correct location and then turned off both lights before she shut the studio door.

"Sit." Bernard pointed to the small sofa.

She complied but asked, "What's going on?"

"The trip to Cannes is required. You will accompany us to a meeting with a very important man. He wants to meet the person who can copy the masters' works so well that they fool the most discerning inspection."

She narrowed her eyes at him. "What? Why?"

"Because you are now a criminal."

Her mouth dropped open. "What?"

"Really, are you so obtuse? Why would we pick only the paintings that are out of circulation, lodged in private vaults around the world? The videos and the pictures we took are... how do you Americans say it? Oui. Blackmail. You've produced a work that has already been validated as authentic. The Pissarro. Those pictures were the only known photograph of the fifth self-portrait of himself. It has been rumored to be in existence for decades. Now it does. Should the authorities find out about your work, you'll go to jail for the rest of your life. The Direction Général de la Sécurité Extérieure frowns on foreign nationals perpetrating massive fraud."

She shook her head and wrapped her arms around herself. "The paint's not old. It will never pass examination."

"We've added a chemical that ages the pigmentation. The canvases you were given are dated accordingly."

She stood and gripped her throat, fear choking her. "I was doing school assignments!"

He threw back his head and laughed. "What an imbecilic notion. We recruited you when you came to attention in the United States. Our contact within the GDSE watches for your type of talent. You were perfect. You have no family. No one to miss you, and you have already been investigated by your own country for replicating the masters. You have a record, yes? You, my dear, are, as the Americans say it, screwed."

She shook her head and stepped back from the man she once thought of as a friend and a mentor. "I have people back in Lake Garden. People who would miss me."

"The old doctor. Yes, yes, this is true. But old women die all the time." He waved his hand in the air, dismissing her statement. "If you do not do exactly what we tell you when we tell you, she will die."

"Do? You mean paint." God, she prayed that was all.

"Yes. You belong to us now. This apartment is yours to use as long as you comply. Should you run or try to warn anyone, well, we will act accordingly. Talib has certain desires for you, little one. He's on a tether now. One misstep and his control will snap. You understand? You will be watched, and your phone, the one I gave you to use in France? It is monitored."

"How can you do this? Why? Oh, my God." She backed into the wall that separated the kitchen and the living area. She jumped at the contact, her breath catching in her throat.

"Money, my dear. Money. We will dictate what you do, where you go, dress you, keep you, yes? You do what we want when we want. If you try anything, we will kill your Maggie. Slowly. There is a new player, too—this Roman. A bad boy who you had a relationship with, this one we will also find. We have contacts everywhere. Roman Alexander will be easy to find."

She jumped as if she'd been shot when he said Roman's last name.

"How?"

"It isn't difficult. Your talent required we find out everything about you. He will die after the old woman. Then we will kill you, but rest assured, you all will die slowly. So very slowly."

Her knees shook and bile rose in her throat. "You can't do this. Please, just let me go home. I won't say a word. I swear." She fell to her knees, no longer able to stand. "Please."

"Ah, if you were less talented, we would send you back to America, yes. We have done so with numerous others. They were not good enough. They submitted their assignments but could not be retained on scholarship." Bernard laughed and walked toward the door. "None had your talent for replicating the masters. You will never see America again, my beauty. Perhaps, if you acquiesce to Talib, you won't be so... lonely, oui?"

"Never." She wanted to scream the word but it came out as a whisper.

Bernard hit the chain on the door. "This will not stop Talib if he decides to act. Remember that. Your future is in your hands. You can work and live or resist and cause the deaths of two people before you are given to Talib. He does have particular tastes that lend to that end. He likes to choke his women as he climaxes. Over and over again. Plus, he loves to abuse his women. He enjoys the pain. Theirs, not his. Finish that painting with the same degree of excellence as you started it with, or your friends will suffer the consequences." He opened the door and walked out.

She sank to her butt, shaking violently. "Oh, God." She stared up at the ceiling. "Please, please, help me." She sobbed the words, but the only response was the echoing sound of her own ignorance. How had she been so stupid?

"Babe. Come here." Jewell motioned for Zane.

He kicked the floor while seated in his desk chair and rolled over to her console. "What's up?"

"Might be a problem. We had an alert on Roman Alexander. It's the real name for Sunset Operative Fourteen."

Zane leaned forward. "Who's looking for Reaper?"

"That's just it, I'm not sure. It came in the form of a missing persons report out of Lake Garden, Pennsylvania."

"He's been in the program for at least ten years. Why the report now?"

Jewell lifted her head. "I don't know. I can't see beyond what's here."

Zane blinked up at her. "That was a rhetorical question, sweetheart."

"Oh. Anyway, do you want to call Kaeden, or do you want me to do it? The Sunset Operatives are your and his jurisdiction."

"I'll do it." He leaned forward and kissed his wife. "Send that to my system, please."

Jewell tapped a few keystrokes and nodded. "Done. I should get a treat for that."

Zane chuckled and reached into the refrigerator that lived under the long worktable. "You know you can have a candy bar occasionally." He handed her a bar with peanuts, caramel, and nougat.

"My favorite!" She unwrapped the brown paper and took a bite, talking as she chewed. "If I have one every time I want one, I'll be as big as a house. This way, it's special."

He checked to make sure he had the document pulled up before he answered. "Your mind amazes me in the best possible way." Zane chuckled and realized he'd lost his wife to her systems. She leaned over the desk with the candy bar held in her teeth as she typed.

He shook his head and grabbed the phone. When Anubis answered, he gave him the information he'd been given.

"Fuck. Not a good time for this. He has an op in France. Is this a singular probe?"

"At this point in time, yes." He'd make sure Jewell tightened the monitoring around Reaper although he'd bet his next paycheck that she already had a virtual fence around the man.

"All right. I don't have any reason to pull him off the case right now. I'll get ahold of Smoke. If there is a reason someone would be looking for him, Smoke should know. We'll handle it from here. Keep me posted on anything further.

"You know it, my friend. Whatever it takes."

"As long as it takes, my brother. Annex out."

CHAPTER 5

Reaper looked at the phone and smiled as he swiped the face and answered the call. "Hello, old man, how's married life treating you?"

"I'm not old, and it is freaking awesome, you should try it."

Just like that, his humor deflated. "Not likely." He'd never marry because only one woman had the key to his heart. Hell, to his soul. Everyone else he'd ever been with had been a distraction or a means to scratch an itch. Nameless and faceless except for Val, and hell, that was just a one-night stand. Neither one of them had ever mentioned it since it happened all those years ago. They were better as friends. Way better.

"Don't knock it until you try it, but this isn't a social call. We had a probe into your past."

Reaper dropped his feet, straddling the beach lounger he was relaxing on, and sat up. "Explain that." He glanced around the crowded beach. No one was paying any attention to him, but he wasn't going to take any chances.

"Single probe, missing persons report on you from Lake Garden. Any people there that might want to find you?"

"No." He'd seen Maggie when he'd last been home and that had been months ago, before his last mission. "Unless the event is being pushed." The event was what the Shadows called the way Demos had found them.

"I'm thinking no. Wouldn't that be more of a wanted for questioning type situation?"

He shook his head. "Yeah. I've got no one back there." Maggie wouldn't look for him. If she'd passed and left him something, lawyers would be looking for him, and not with a missing persons report. Harmony? He glanced down the beach, seeing all the blondes on the beach. She was lost to him. Forever.

"What about that girl you talked about?"

Reaper chuffed out a sound. "You have a damn good memory."

"I do. Answer the question." Smoke's smart-ass response was familiar ground for him.

He leaned back in the chair and put his feet up on the lounger. "She's in Paris now. She received a full-ride scholarship to an art institute or something…" He glanced around again. "But there was something fishy. The initial contact was because she entered a contest that I was told she didn't remember entering." Smoke's silence on the other end made him look at the phone to see if they were still connected. "If you think I'm being stupid and reaching for straws, say so. The silent treatment isn't amusing."

"No, no, I never discount anything that rings strange to any of us. I was looking for my… oh, there it is. Tell me her name and everything you can remember. I'll have CCS run it to the ground."

Reaper lowered his voice and made sure no one was within listening range before he gave Harmony's name, date of birth, and a detailed synopsis of what Maggie had told him. The man repeated everything he said word for word. The new speech-to-dictation program Smoke had made it easier for the man to adapt to his inability to read or write well. He'd come clean to Reaper after he and Charley had gotten engaged. Reaper shrugged the news off; he'd known for a while, but that act of not caring meant a lot to Smoke. He could tell.

"Send to CCS, attention Zane Reynolds. Okay. That's done. In the meantime, Anubis mentioned you were active. Anything you need from me?"

"Not at the moment, but I'll call if I do." He wasn't active in the mission until tomorrow at the earliest. Val and the others Guardian had sent to Cannes were eyes-deep in the op. He was just biding his time and waiting for the green light.

"All right, my friend. Keep yourself out of trouble."

Reaper chuckled. "That's my line."

"What? Are you insinuating that I'm anything less than an outstanding operative with a stellar record?"

"Let's see... should we talk about the time off the coast of Costa Rica?"

"What was that? You're breaking up. Can't hear you. Gotta go! Whatever it takes." The call disconnected.

Reaper chuckled and dropped the phone on his lap. *As long as it takes.* He drew a breath and scanned the beach again. He'd had enough people watching. It was time to get showered and find a place to eat.

The bistro on Rue Louis Blanc, recommended by the concierge, was a pleasant surprise. Quiet even though it was just off the busy tourist area, the lack of stimulation was what he needed after a day of sun on the beach. He ordered the foie gras for his appetizer, pairing a crisp white wine to complement the fattiness of the duck. He'd come from very humble roots, but he'd learned to become anything his mission required him to be. He was comfortable rubbing elbows with the world's elite or sharing a burn barrel's warmth with the homeless. He now spoke French, Italian, and proper English. His Spanish was… passable, but he was working on it. His abilities allowed him to meld with the natives of these languages. A shadow amongst the inhabitants.

After his appetizer was cleared, his main course of medallions of prime beef, artichokes, and cherries served with a mushroom cream sauce arrived. He paired it with a heavy merlot. Every bite was an explosion of flavor. Dessert featured fresh peaches, pain de géne biscuit, compote, and a rich vanilla ice cream. He leaned back in his chair while savoring his coffee. The perks of his job sometimes amazed him. The pay and the education were beyond anything he'd expected when Demos had found him. Hell, he would have been happy to have had enough to buy his uncle's farm. Now, he had millions in offshore accounts, and a vault full of aliases, cash, and enough weapons to start a small war. Guardian was his salvation, and his loyalty would always be with them.

He paid for his meal, leaving the anticipated tip. Anything that would draw attention to himself—overtipping, undertipping, sending food back—was avoided at all costs. Kind, impersonal, and politely disinterested in conversation greyed his presence even more. Just another plate to be served. His height he could do nothing about, but tall men were in abundance in these busy cities.

He strolled back to the hotel, running the blueprints of Ardan's fortress through his mind again. Very few cars passed by at this time of night. Two black sedans turned onto the street and had to stop to wait for pedestrians to clear the road. He ambled past, casting a glance at the second car. His heart stopped, and he froze.

Harmony?

The woman's head jerked around, and she stared at him. She looked terrified. *Of him? Fuck.* He was only able to grab the last numbers of the license plate before it moved forward and was out of sight on the dark street. He glanced at his watch and noted the time and the street name the car traveled. He'd get the information to Anubis. If there were any street cameras, Guardian could access them and get the rest of the plate. His oh-shit meter was now officially pegged.

Forcing himself to continue to his hotel rather than running through the streets of Cannes chasing that car was one of the hardest things he'd done in the last ten years, and he'd been through hell and back in that time. He'd learned how to deal with unexpected events. He smiled politely to the doorman of his hotel, waited for the elevator without exploding, and slowly walked down the hall to his room. He checked his countermeasures to ensure the room hadn't been entered. The thread he shut at knee height was still there. The other devices were also unaltered.

He removed his suit jacket and his tie, unbuttoned the top button of his shirt, and unfastened his cufflinks before he crossed the room and poured himself a glass of single malt. He retrieved his phone and sat down at the table, looking out at the night sky. Inky blackness stared back at him. He closed his eyes and replayed every facet of the ten-second interaction. It was her. There was no doubt in his mind. Her hair was longer, her face fuller and softer, but those big hazel eyes had connected with his. Her shell-shocked expression at seeing him had to have mirrored his. It was the fear in her eyes, the unadulterated fear, that worried him. What in the hell was going on?

He took a drink of his scotch and drew a deep breath. He hit the digits he knew by heart. Operative cell phones did not save numbers nor were numbers logged in the call data. If anyone were to take a phone, they'd learn exactly zero about the operative or the calls they made. Texts were a different story. As they were typed, they were scrambled. If you didn't know the code to unscramble the message, you didn't read the text. If anyone tried to enter the code incorrectly, the phone would fry itself. He'd learned fast to pay attention to changing codes. It was hell to operate without a phone even for a short time.

"Operator Two-Seven-Four."

"Send me to the Annex. Priority Dusk."

"Stand by." The operator responded in the same unflustered calm with which she always responded. Phoenix swore he had a conversation with the woman while he was waiting to be connected to Doc Wheeler. He said she was nice and asked questions. Personally, he thought Phoenix was off his rocker. The woman had never been anything but professional and... distant to him. Almost robotic.

"Authenticate Shallow." Anubis' voice came across the connection.

"Grave," he automatically replied.

"Sitrep." Anubis knew he wouldn't call unless it was important.

"I talked to our mutual friend, the boat captain, today."

"I am aware."

"Tonight, as I was leaving a restaurant, I saw the subject of his inquiry."

"Did the subject see you?"

"Affirm."

"Recognition?"

"Guaranteed. I have a partial license plate and direction and time of travel." He listed off the information.

"This could be coincidental," Anubis mused as he heard the sound of his handler typing.

"There's something else. Intangible. Subject was terrified."

"Explain that."

"I can't. I just know it."

"There has been no contact since your inception?"

"No, none." He'd made sure of it.

"I'll take it from here. You're still on hold unless

you hear from CoC." His chain of command, meaning Anubis was passing this up the line.

"Affirmative. Out."

"Hey." Anubis' call caught him before he hung up.

"Yes?"

"Where's your head?"

"I'm confused and curious but on point."

"We'll figure it out. Whatever it takes."

"Roger that. As long as it takes." He cleared the line and sat his phone down. He picked up his drink and walked to the window. The lights that lined the boulevard below illuminated people out for a late-night stroll. He followed a couple from one point of light to the next. *What had happened to put that fear into her eyes?* He lifted his scotch and stared at the dark amber liquid as he swirled it in his crystal goblet. The feelings he'd pushed down surfaced again. Only this time, he couldn't drive to Lake Garden to check on her, to threaten Delbert, or send her anonymous gifts. He drank the rest of his scotch and put the tumbler down on the bar. He'd lived Guardian's credo for the last ten years; he was counting on them to come through for him this time. Smoke knew how important Harmony was to him. A couple years ago, they'd had an all-night conversation over a bottle of rotgut, and he'd talked about the one who got away. Or rather, the one he left.

There was nothing to do now but wait for information or a green light. Either way, letting the past haunt the future was counterproductive. He gathered all the questions, concerns, and even worry, and shoved them back into the small space in his mind he'd allotted them. He couldn't let the distraction of Harmony and what was happening interfere with the mission. If he did, he could die. And then what good would he be to Harmony? None.

Reaper closed his eyes and turned his neck, literally cracking the tension out of his body. He used every technique that he'd been taught and turned off his emotions. He wasn't Roman Alexander any longer. He was Reaper, and as an assassin, he had no connection to Harmony Flinn. He rolled his shoulders, started a detailed run-through of his tentative operation tomorrow night, and ignored the pain as another piece of his past withered.

CHAPTER 6

"What are you looking at?" Talib turned and gazed out the rear window of the vehicle.

"There's a restaurant. I'm hungry." Harmony swiveled, facing forward. *Oh, my God! Oh, my God!* She closed her eyes and wrapped her arms around her stomach. *That was Roman.* It had to have been Roman. He recognized her, didn't he? Dear Lord, what was he doing in Cannes? Maggie said that he had lied to her and told her he worked overseas. What if he was telling the truth?

"The hotel isn't far. You can order room service," Bernard said from the front seat.

"What?" Bernard's statement pulled her out of her spiral.

"Food." Talib drawled the word and then turned

back, looking out the rear window. "I have a feeling food wasn't what attracted your attention."

She turned her head and glared at the bastard. "Unlike you, there are some people who actually function normally and don't think of sex every other second."

Talib snarled, "How did you know I was thinking of sex?"

Bernard laughed heartily while he responded. "It's all you think about. We will get you food at the hotel."

Harmony made some noise of agreement. She probably wouldn't be able to eat a bite. She had been able to eat hardly anything since Bernard had dropped his nuclear bomb on her world. Everything had exploded, and the fallout wasn't even close to settling. She was a criminal. Unsuspecting and unwilling, true, but a criminal, nonetheless. She packed the fancy clothes made of silk and fine fabrics as she was instructed. She wore what she was told. Talib and Bernard made her dance like a bear at a circus. Neither she nor the bear wanted to perform, yet both were unable to say no.

The line she would draw was with Talib. She would not tolerate any physical contact. If they wanted paintings, she wanted him away from her. It would be her line in the sand if she could get Bernard to agree to her terms. Talib's words, gestures, unwanted touches, and gazes all told her that he was ready to pounce at a moment's notice.

She followed Bernard and Talib into the hotel foyer. The majesty of the resort should have enthralled her. It didn't. The grandeur registered as small and insignificant. The opulence barely registered as thoughts of Roman raced through her mind. *My God, how he had changed.* So much larger than he was when she had last seen him. His hair was styled and the clothes he wore looked expensive. That strong jawline and straight nose still punctuated the handsomeness of his face. She would know him anywhere. Even here on the coast of France. She prayed that he didn't live here. Hopefully, he didn't recognize her. Although she knew in her heart he had. Perhaps her prayer should be that he didn't try to find her. Talib and Bernard could never know that Roman was here.

"Harmony."

She jolted and stared at Bernard. "What?"

"I said follow us." The anger in Bernard's eyes was something she didn't want escalated.

"I'm sorry, I'm tired and I'm hungry. I was distracted."

"Obviously." Talib extended his hand for her to walk ahead of him. She hated that, but she followed Bernard. Every time she looked over her shoulder, Talib was looking at her like she was the last drop of wine and he was a raging alcoholic. Her skin crawled at the thought of him ever touching her. She'd do what these bastards wanted until she could find a way to escape. There had to be a way.

"This is your room. It is connected to mine. The connecting door will be open at all times. If you leave, try to call out on the telephone, or do anything that would compromise our agreement, you know what will happen." Bernard turned and looked at Talib as he spoke.

Talib leaned in and sniffed her neck. "Is that fear I smell?"

"More like revulsion." Harmony walked through the doors into her room. The entryway to the hall was shut behind her and she heard Bernard enter his room. The connecting doors were opened immediately.

"What do you want ordered from room service?" Bernard leaned against the wall.

"You choose." She jumped at the knock from the hallway.

Bernard walked across the small area and opened

the door. The bellman stood with her luggage. When directed, he entered and put her cases in her room. Bernard tipped the man and he exited without comment. "You will want to freshen up after our trip. I will order your food. You can lock that." He pointed to the main entrance. "I know you do not trust Talib to stay out." Bernard laughed as he walked back through the connecting doors.

Harmony sank down onto her bed and held her head in her hands. How was she going to live like this? A small voice inside her spoke, '*One day at a time*.' Her aunt's words came back to her. Yes, she'd live one day at a time and spend every waking moment that she wasn't painting looking for a way out.

After her shower, she dressed in the bathroom and made her way to the open doorway. The fabulous smell of bacon beckoned her. Bernard motioned at her to come in. "They had American breakfast listed as an option. Bacon, potatoes, eggs." He made a disgusted sound in the back of his throat. "Who would clog their stomach with such rubbish is beyond me."

Harmony took the silver domed plate off the cart, grabbed a fork and knife and a glass of orange juice, and walked back to her bedroom. She sat down at the little table that was in the corner of her room and lifted the dome. She took a piece of the crispy bacon and snapped off a small portion. Placing it on her tongue, she closed her eyes and recalled precious thoughts of home and Sunday morning breakfast. Her aunt and uncle had always had bacon, hash browns, and eggs for Sunday breakfast. The plate in front of her was like a lightning rod in the emotional storm surrounding her. She slowly ate what she could and wiped the tears from her face. She wouldn't give Bernard the satisfaction of knowing she was crying. In order to get out of this mess she needed to be hard, she needed to learn to be like them. To be cold, to be calculating, and to be ready to escape at a moment's notice. They could hold the threat of Maggie and Roman over her, but sooner or later, she would find a way out. Harmony looked at the knife in her hand. Yes, she'd make them pay, too. Another emotion surfaced. This one was one she would embrace, and she'd keep it in front of her night and day.

Vengeance.

Jewell sat at her monitor and stared at the letters and numbers in front of her. "Something's not right." She leaned forward and pulled a pencil out of her messy bun. "Where did you actually end up?" She put the pencil between her teeth and started typing. Twenty-five minutes later, she was back in her chair. She lifted the receiver of her phone and pushed a button. "Hey, Sonya, this is Jewell, is the big guy around?"

"He is on another call right now. Do you need me to interrupt?" Sonya knew that she wouldn't call unless it was an emergency.

Jewell pulled her bottom lip between her teeth and looked at the information she had uncovered. "It's important; the thing is I'm not sure how important it is. Could you just have him come down here when he's done with the telephone call?"

Sonya laughed. "With pleasure. That man stays inside that office from sunup to sundown. I'll get a crowbar and send him your way."

Jewell chuckled as she hung up. She turned back to the computer monitor and shook her head. "You don't fit into my puzzle. Maybe you fit somewhere else..." She spoke to herself as she went over the information again. She'd bet money on it. *Oh, that's it!*

She jolted when Jason entered her office. "Wow, that was fast."

Jason's brow creased. "It's been an hour and a half since you called." He moved over to her console and peered over her shoulder. "What are you working on to make you lose track of time?"

"If you asked my husband? Anything." Jewell chuckled and waved at Zane's empty chair. "He's gone over to see Mrs. Henshaw. He gets itchy when too many days go by. I still want to string up her children."

Jason put his hands in his pockets and rocked back on his heels. "We take care of her, it's all we can do. You can't force others' familial relationships. Now, what did you call me down here for?"

"Oh, right. Kaeden sent over some information that Dan gave him. Following the bouncing ball so far?" Jewell glanced up at her brother. He nodded. "Okay, so this old flame of Sunset Operative Fourteen got a full ride scholarship to an art school in Paris. The only problem is this school doesn't exist." She clicked her mouse a couple times and nodded to the website on her monitor. "It looks legit, and on the surface, it is. But not when you dig."

Jason reached for Zane's chair and pulled it over so he could sit down. "I missed a bounce."

"Which one?" Jewell had tried to make it crayon level. Damn it, she hated when she lost people.

"Why are we digging into Fourteen's past?" Jason leaned forward and stared at her.

"Oh, guess you didn't get that brief. Don't kill the messenger. Okay?" Jewell took a pencil out of her hair and twirled it nervously in her fingers. She hated when she got ahead of the section heads. "If they didn't think it was important enough to send up to you, maybe this is nothing." She looked at the monitor and then shook her head. "Only it's not nothing. Damn, I wish Zane was here. I wouldn't have jumped the gun then."

Jason put his hand on her forearm. "Button, you didn't do anything wrong. Just tell me what you were going to tell me, and I'll contact his handlers and get the rest of the information. If you think it's important, I need to know it. So, start from the beginning and make it crayon level simple for me, will you? It's been one of those days."

"Do you ever have any other kind of day?" She made a face at him.

He laughed a bit. "I do when I'm with my family. They're my touchstone, just like you are for me here. So, what do you need to tell me?"

"Okay, so yesterday, or maybe the day before—

I'm not sure, the days can run together—Godzilla got a hit on a missing persons report filed on Roman Alexander. Which is way weird because it came from his hometown, and he left there ten years ago. We were able to intercept and delete the report. The issuing authority will never know what has been done. But that's not all. See, I got information from Kaeden. It seems that this past love interest of Fourteen's entered a contest and won a full scholarship to a private art school in Paris."

Jason's eyebrow lifted. "I smell fish."

"I'd say you smell an entire cannery. I was able to find Harmony Flinn's old email account. It wasn't difficult once I isolated the IP addresses of Lake Garden, Pennsylvania. It was a simple search and destroy mission, looking for anything that would key on Harmony or Flinn or any combination of her name. Getting in was easy; her password was Fourteen's birthday backwards. I'll give her props for that. Anywho, I was able to find the email that she had received from the school. It went back to this website." She pointed at the monitor. "Follow me so far?"

"I'm with you." Jason motioned for her to go ahead.

"Well, I went to look at the financials of the

school. There are none. They have no presence in France." Jewell crossed her arms, leaned back in her chair and looked at her brother.

"Where do they have a financial presence?" Jason narrowed his eyes at her.

"Ah, you see, that's why you're the boss man. I traced this website to the entity who posted it. Not impossible to do, but very difficult. I mean candy bar difficult if you get my drift."

Jason leaned back in the chair, opened the refrigerator, and grabbed two candy bars. He offered one to her and unwrapped his. "Continue." He took a large bite of the bar.

She continued as she unwrapped hers. "His name is Talib Behar. He's a citizen of Monaco who currently resides in Paris. His daddy is Barack Behar." She took a bite of her candy bar and watched her brother's reaction.

Jason swallowed the bite he was chewing and smiled. "This just keeps getting better and better. What is our good friend Barack's son doing in Paris? And how is he linked to the website? Does he have an art degree?"

"That would be a big negative. From the little digging I've done, Talib doesn't *do* anything. He has three residences in Paris. One he lives in; of course, it is in the most affluent and elite portion of Paris. The second is a two-thousand-square-foot apartment at the city center. The third is a very small crappy apartment near the town center."

"He's keeping a mistress or two." Jason took another bite of his candy bar and spoke around the chocolate, "Not a crime."

"Yeah, I know. But then, I asked myself why he would pay for this website and also pay for its maintenance. What could he benefit from? So, I took a look around the website. It claims this school, which doesn't exist, offers scholarships to artists around the world who want to learn the exacting techniques of Impressionist era masters. That, my brother, jogged something in my brain from when I read Harmony's file. It would seem that Miss Flinn's cousin, Delbert Anders, tried to sell one of Harmony's paintings to someone in Pittsburgh, claiming it was an original. The person who answered the Craigslist ad contacted the FBI. It seems that the Monet that Miss Flinn had painted was currently on display at the Met. Good old Delbert wanted a whopping fifteen hundred dollars for the painting. The FBI investigated. Delbert took that painting without permission from his cousin. She signed the painting on the back with her name. The FBI indicated the copy was nearly flawless, but Miss Flinn wasn't complicit in her cousin's stupidity. He got probation for trying to pawn off the painting as real."

"Who are Talib Behar's known associates?" Jason popped the last of his candy bar into his mouth.

"That would be the question of the day, big brother. May I introduce you to Bernard LaVette, a man of ill repute? Care to guess what the French police have investigated him for?"

"Art fraud?" Jason licked some chocolate off his finger.

Jewell took another bite of her candy bar and shook her head. "Nope, but close. He *was* one of the foremost authorities of Impressionist art. He fell from grace when he authenticated not one but two works of art which were later proven to be frauds. The French police investigated and found a money trail between Bernard and the offshore account where the funds were transferred for the original purchase. They couldn't prove anything else, but it was enough. The press crucified him, and he lost all credibility in the art world. Care to guess how many shell companies I had to go through in order to find out who owned that account that paid him for his appraisals?"

"I wouldn't want to spoil the surprise. How many?" Jason leaned back and crossed his arms.

"Thirty-seven. And let me tell you, at number thirty-one, I was ready to give up," Jewell snickered. "But I didn't. Talib Behar's now-defunct company, the one that went bankrupt five years ago, I forget the name..." She leaned forward to look at her screen.

"Beacon." Jason supplied the name for her.

"Yeah, that's it. Well, that company was listed as one of the shareholders of the shell company. With that bit of information, I was able to link the other four companies back to not only Baby Behar but also Papa Behar. But that's not the kicker here. Ask me who else Talib rubs elbows with and to whom I also linked the account." Jewell took a bite of her candy bar. "Maybe this was a two-candy bar effort," she mumbled to herself.

"Who?" Jason reached back to the fridge and grabbed two bottles of water, handing her one.

She took it and lifted it in a toast. "Chevalier Ardan."

Jason froze. The only things that moved were his eyes behind his glasses as he put the case together with the other information she'd worked for the Council months ago. "Untraceable currency, perhaps, but why would the Behars work with Ardan?" Jason stood up. "You did good, Button. Order in a pizza and tell Zane I said you earned it." He reached down and hugged her so tight he nearly lifted her out of her chair.

When he released her, she wiggled back into her seat and asked, "Wait, so, what does this have to do with Harmony Flinn and Fourteen?"

"Damn good question. Which line goes to the Annex?"

Jewell handed him the receiver and pushed the button. She then promptly rolled over to Zane's console and dialed a number she knew by heart. "Hey, Leo, this is Jewell. I know, right? A long time. I want an extra-large triple meat, double cheese pizza. Oh, throw a couple veggies on there, too, okay? No, I don't care what kind, I won't eat them anyway. It makes my husband happy when I order them, though. Yep. I'll let the guys know it's coming."

She turned around and watched the door closing behind Jason. "Bye!" She called after him. She grabbed a pencil off her workspace and shoved it in her hair. "Candy *and* a pizza." She stared at the information she'd found. "I should have asked for an energy drink, too."

CHAPTER 7

R eaper jolted from sleep and grabbed his phone. He swiped the face and answered, immediately awake. Before he could say anything, the operator spoke.

"Stand by for conference call." She repeated the phrase each time someone picked up the phone. By the sound of it, something was fucked up with his mission.

"Archangel, all parties are online. Operator Two-Seven-Four is clear."

The big boss' gravelly voice asked, "Jewell, are we secure?"

"Locked up tight." Her response was immediate.

"Good. We have the Rose, the Annex, CCS, and

Dom Ops on the call along with Sunset Operatives Thirteen and Fourteen."

Reaper's brow creased. *Thirteen?* Why was Val on the call? Were they going to pull him from the mission and give the primary to Val?

"There have been some developments in the mission. Ardan's sanctioned code is on hold. We have confirmed established links between Ardan and Talib and Barack Behar. Behar has been on our scope for ten years. Recently, it has been rumored Behar has funded coups in several third-world countries."

"The Caribbean?" Reaper asked.

"No. We have no evidence of his participation, but the connection to Ardan isn't a coincidence based on Ardan's recent role in the supply of arms to the area. If Ardan is the muscle supplying the arms and Behar is the one pulling his strings, we want to know," Archangel explained. "The Council is in unanimous agreement that further investigation is warranted. Thirteen, were you able to contact Ardan?"

Val's silky laugh made him smile. "Yes. I gave him my cover name yesterday when we met. His body-guard came by my suite this afternoon and asked if I'd like to attend an art exhibit with him tonight. I said I'd think about it, and after he left, I checked into it and found next to nothing on it; however, the guard did say it would be held at a local chapel."

Reaper glanced out the window. The sun had just started to throw golden hues across the eastern horizon.

"I'm taking that it isn't a public event?" Archangel asked.

"I was told the event was invitation-only," Val replied.

"Jewell, we need an invite issued to Fourteen using his current profile. Find out who is organizing this event and get me some leverage."

"On it. We have an ace up our sleeve on the art thingy, it shouldn't be a problem. And we can confirm Ardan ran a background on Thirteen's cover. He was good. We're better," Jewell quipped in response.

Archangel continued, "Perfect. Dom Ops, bring us up to speed."

"Roger that. Based on our initial investigation, we believe that Harmony Flinn was duped by an elaborate scheme to utilize her unique talents to copy some of the best masters' work."

Reaper closed his eyes and dropped his head. *Fuck.* Someone had used her dream of painting to lure her into a web of criminals. No wonder fear laced her expression last night. "She's in trouble. I saw it in her eyes last night."

"She very well could be. We sent an investigator up to Lake Garden to speak with Doctor Cooper. She was hesitant to answer our questions at first because someone else had been there three days prior asking about Roman Alexander and his connection to Harmony Flinn. The doctor stated she downplayed the link between the two of you, but anyone who was questioned in town would confirm the connection." The man in Dom Ops paused for a moment before he continued. "Dr. Cooper also said as of two weeks ago she hadn't heard from Harmony, which was unusual as they talked at least once a week. The last time they talked, Harmony was concerned about the advances of one of the men her professor had introduced to her. She didn't know the man's last name, but his first name was Talib."

Reaper's upper lip drew up in a snarl, but he forced himself to pay attention.

"Behar." Archangel finished for Dom Ops. "Talib Behar, or rather, a shell company thirty-seven times removed from the asshole, funded the fake website that was used to recruit her to Paris. A disavowed art expert who specializes in Impressionist-era paint-ings is also involved."

Dom Ops chuckled. "Let me guess, Bernard LaVette."

"Ding, ding, ding," Jewell chirped in.

"That name is one Dr. Cooper did remember. She said LaVette was Harmony's friend and professor."

Some friend. Reaper committed the name to memory. LaVette wouldn't escape this event unscathed.

"How is art fraud connected to overthrowing governments?" Val voiced the question he was thinking.

"That's for you to find out. Thirteen, you now have Ardan as primary. Fourteen, Talib is yours if you can reach him without Ms. Flinn throwing your cover. Get as much information as you can. I want answers. Fourteen, is your cover one which would interest Talib?"

"It is." He was in the presidential suite of one of the most exclusive hotels in the city. His cover made him an international playboy, and his reputation was established in the elite's circle.

Archangel doled out the assignments. "Annex, the mission parameters have been issued, did you receive your copy?"

"Affirmative. I've updated all mission specs and will ensure all involved have new instructions or are reassigned as necessary."

"Perfect. Fury, I want another Sunset asset in-country. I don't care if it is a team or singular asset but get us assistance in the area. Also, send in the medical team. I don't want my assets in-country working around one of the most powerful and bloodthirsty men in the world without medical assistance."

"Roger that. I'll let the Annex know who will be going and coordinate the medical team's travel and positioning with them."

"Good. I'll brief Alpha when he gets back. I want an update tomorrow morning. Archangel out."

"Dom Ops is clear."

"Let me know if you need anything else from me. CCS out." The exit was said in one breath.

Anubis cleared his throat. "Okay, we are on hold for previous mission parameters. Fourteen, confirm acknowledgement of stand down."

"Confirmed, standing down," Reaper responded.

"Stand by," Fury broke in. The line went dead for a moment before he came back and relayed, "Okay, for both of you in the field, CCS is sending background on new players and information on the exhibit."

"I copy."

Anubis broke in. "We are looking for connections between Ardan and both Behars. Fourteen, it is your discretion on contacting Talib when he's around Ms. Flinn. If you believe she will compromise you, don't proceed."

With an aristocratic drawl creeping through his perfect French, Reaper replied. "I'm sorry, madam, but you must have mistaken me for someone else."

Anubis snorted. "That should work. If not, get the hell out and we'll work it with other assets."

Reaper didn't acknowledge the command. If Harmony was in trouble, Guardian would play hell in getting him away from the op. Anubis either didn't notice or knew what was going through his mind because he didn't stop and require an acknowledgement. "Do either of you need anything from us?"

"No," Val replied.

"My cover is solid. I'm good." He liked the man he was portraying, a cover he'd used numerous times, and as Conrad Belmonte, he'd made friends in this circle of the elite. If Talib or Ardan were to inquire about his background, there wouldn't be any problems.

"Find out how the Behars are involved with Ardan and then we'll let you do what you've been trained to do." Fury growled the order before he drawled, "The Rose is clear."

"You know how to contact us if you need anything. Annex Out."

Reaper cleared the call and was just about to set his phone down when it vibrated in his hand. He opened it and glanced at his text icon. He opened the program and saw the gibberish that was delivered. He hit the star on his keypad and entered his code.

> *You okay?*

He smiled at the text. Val was checking up on him.

> *GTG*

He knew that wouldn't hold the woman, but he had to laugh. He was good to go and very, very ready to find out what the hell was happening.

> *Sigh... do I need to come over there and beat the shit out of you?*

He actually laughed at the threat. She was good, but she couldn't take him. No one could. He was a close quarters expert. Fighting dirty was his hall-mark. Killing with a garrote was his calling card. No one could fight death, not when the reaper had your name.

>*You could try. This is personal.*

> *How personal?*

>*TOIL*

The one I left. TOIL, what a perfect acronym. He'd labored over his decision to leave Harmony every day for the past ten years.

>*Still love her?*

>*Still love him?*

There wasn't a response. Val hadn't left her man; he'd been killed. Her code name was more than just a mythical Norse angel. Val, in every aspect, was the woman who decided who died on the battlefield she was assigned. A true spearmaiden of lore, she used a dagger with exacting precision, usually at the base of her victim's skull, angled into the brain. A quick and brutal death. She was a merciless assassin who killed with an eagerness that, at times, was barely harnessed.

His phone rang, and he switched apps to answer it. "Yes?"

"She is important. We will save her and then worry about the assignment."

Val's words spread a sad smile across his lips. He shook his head even though she couldn't see him. "You don't need to get involved in this, my friend."

There was a moment of silence before she responded. "I have nine friends. You're one of them. I would do anything for you."

"And I you, but at this point, we don't know what is involved. Making plans now is useless."

"I know you're right, but I want to do something. I'm bored." Val pouted out the words and he laughed.

"Don't you have a dress to go buy?"

She sighed. "No, I have the perfect dress. It will have Ardan eating out of my hand."

"What about shoes?"

"Louboutins. Perfect."

"Purse?" He chuckled.

"Swarovski crystal-beaded Louis Vuitton clutch."

Reaper chuckled. "I got nothing else."

"You forgot the best part—the lingerie," Val chuckled.

"I'm assuming you have that taken care of, too."

"Indeed. Now, tell me about you and this woman."

"Why should I tell you that?" Reaper countered.

"I told you, I'm bored."

He laughed, "I don't exist for your amusement."

"You mean all of our history has been dumb luck?"

"Obviously." He drew out the word and they both laughed.

"Seriously, if she's involved in this op, I want to know everything I can learn about her. You might not be able to contact her, and if you have to bail from the visible part of this mission, then I want information to help me."

Reaper drew a deep breath and checked the face of the phone again to make sure their call was secure. The little red flashing light on the face told him it was. "Harmony and I met when she was five and I was seven. I moved to Lake Garden to live with my father's best friend after my old man was murdered. I saw her older cousin whipping her with a branch in the woods that joined their farm and the farm where I was living. I pushed the idiot down and threatened to kick his ass if he lifted a hand to her again. From then on, Harmony and I were best friends, then we dated and, finally, were lovers."

"Why did you leave?" Val's question held a depth of emotion that only a fellow Shadow would understand. What was his tipping point? What turned him into a killer?

He didn't hesitate to tell her. "Lake Garden has

four hundred people on a good day. It's a typical small town. One or two families run the place. In Lake Garden, it was the Grahams. Bert Graham wanted Tom's land. Tom is the name of the man who raised me. He offered Tom money. When that didn't work, he tried to claim Tom was arrear in his taxes, which also failed because Tom kept damn good records. Then Bert cut his water off from the land upstream that he owned. A real asshole. Tom drilled a well and life went on. I was away at a football game when Bert claimed he and Tom went hunting. Tom wouldn't be within a country mile of Bert let alone go hunting with the man. Tom was shot in the back. Bert claimed it was an accident, that he stumbled on something and fell, the weapon discharged. Since the Grahams ran the town, there wasn't an investigation. It was labeled an accident and Bert bought Tom's farm as soon as the county declared he could because the will leaving it to me turned up missing. I wasn't blood relation so I couldn't just inherit it without the will. The judge who declared Bert could buy the land from the county was kind enough to give me until I graduated to leave the land. Bert Graham turned up at Tom's to gloat one afternoon. He'd been drinking." He could recall it like it happened ten minutes ago, not ten years...

"Why are you here? The judge said I could stay until graduation." He doubted he could stay that long. He didn't have any money, and the food in the house that neighbors had been dropping by was running out, but he'd damn well stay as long as he could just so the bastard in front of him didn't get the land one second sooner.

Bert sauntered up to the porch and pulled a handgun. It was eerie, but everything seemed to slow down and sharpen in his mind. He didn't feel fear. It was uncanny how things crystalized as he watched Bert pull the hammer of his old revolver back.

"I finally got rid of that waste of skin. I tried to make him leave, but no, that son of a bitch wouldn't take the money. Said he was going to make sure you had something when he finally bit it."

Roman cocked his head. Of course. *"You took the will."*

"Why would I go to all the trouble of killing him and getting rid of your old man only to let you inherit?"

"What?" He straightened and took two steps forward, his fists clenched at his side.

"You heard me. This land is going to be a vacation development with restaurants and bars. Big money is going to come spend time here and I'm going to be rich. I have the right people with the money in hand ready to break ground. My land."

"You killed both of them?" He moved forward two more steps.

Bert lifted the gun, but his hand was shaking. "Kid, you're stupid. Tom and your old man were fucking each other."

He blinked at the information. "Why did you kill my dad?" He grasped for any reason until... all those rumors, were they true? Could it be that Bert was gay? He never paid attention, but if he was... "That's why you're not married. You what... wanted... or maybe loved my dad or maybe Tom, didn't you?"

Bert snarled, "Stop! Your father had his chance. I'm going to kill you and claim you came after me. No loose ends, no one to go to court or to ask stupid questions."

Roman flew at the bastard. His left hand struck the gun, sending it flying into the dirt, and his right uppercut slammed into the man's face. The man didn't get up, but Roman's pain and rage kept him swinging. He didn't stop until he was too exhausted to lift his fist again. He sat straddled over the body, pulling ragged gasps of air into his lungs.

"What did you do?" Harmony's horrified gasp lifted his head.

"He killed Tom and my dad, he told me he did. He had a gun, and he was going to kill me, then say that I attacked him." Roman stumbled as he stood and tried to point toward where the gun laid, but his hands were so swollen he couldn't move his fingers. His lungs still heaved, trying to pump enough oxygen into his body. He glanced down at the man he'd beaten to a pulp. "I'll call the sheriff."

"No!" Harmony shook her head and grabbed his arm. "You can't tell anyone, Roman. They'll put you in jail forever."

He was going to puke. Swallowing hard, he rasped, "I killed him, babe. I have to pay for that."

"Tom and your dad already paid, this damn town don't get to have you, too. Help me get him into his car. We can take the dirt roads and drive him up the mountain, hide him and his car, and climb down."

"Harmony, if you do anything but call to report this, you're an accomplice." He'd wanted to be a police officer when he graduated. They had academies he could join at eighteen, he'd looked it up on the computers at the library at school. That dream dissolved in front of his eyes.

She took a step toward him. She didn't wipe at the tears that streaked her face. "Not if you don't get caught. We don't say anything and keep our heads down. Now, come on!" She grabbed one of Bert's boots and started tugging on it. Her little five feet, five inch body tugged him about an inch before Roman bent down and placed a bloody, swollen hand on her forearm.

"Harmony, stop."

She dropped to her knees, sobbing. "You didn't mean to kill him. I know it. You shouldn't go to jail."

He sat down at the feet of the man he'd beaten to death and pulled her into his lap. As she cried, he stared at what he'd done. He didn't feel remorse for killing the man. He was an evil being who'd done horrible things. No, instead, he held his regret in his arms. He'd have to leave Lake Garden—and leave her. Not that people wouldn't figure out what had happened, but Harmony was right. He'd load Bert into his car and drive him back to that monstrosity of a house where the man lived alone. Then he'd hit the road. If he was lucky, he could hitch a ride and get out of town. He buried his face in Harmony's sandy-blonde hair and held her as she cried.

"Please, Roman. Let's just run away."

He shook his head. "I can't make you pay for something I've done, and if you go with me or ever admit you know what happened, they'll try to blame you, too. Go home, baby. I have some things to do."

"What?" She stared up at him.

"I'm not sure yet. Go home, I'll call you when I can." He could tell she didn't believe him.

"I love you. You're all I have. Please, Roman."

She was begging him for something he couldn't give her, and he couldn't give it to her because she was all he *had, too. He'd dreamed of a quiet life with Harmony, with kids and dogs and all the struggles of just getting by, because that was all he knew, but it was enough because he'd have her.* "I love you. More than you could ever understand." *He dropped a soft kiss against her lips.* "Go home. Go before someone figures out you came over." *He stood up and helped her to her feet.*

"Roman?" *She shook her head.*

"Go. I love you." *He stepped back from her and nodded in the direction of the path that had long ago been worn between the two farms.*

She sobbed, spun on her heel, and sprinted away. He watched her as far as he could see her. That was the last time they'd talked.

"You still there?" Val's question broke him from the past.

"Yeah. He admitted to killing my dad and Tom. I beat the bastard to death. Harmony came over just after and saw what I'd done. She begged me to run and take her with me. I couldn't. She couldn't pay the price for my crime. She hasn't seen or spoken to me since."

"Yet you still love her after all this time." It wasn't a question.

"I do. I always will."

"Soul mates," Val whispered.

He didn't argue the point. They were, or at least, in his mind, they had been. "Harmony loved to paint. Her aunt and uncle had this set of encyclopedias and she'd see a picture in the book and be able to recreate it. She loved the Impressionist era because the light became the focus and the scene the backdrop for the light. She's like that for me. She's my light."

"And they are using her talent against her." Val tsked. "But why? For what possible reason do they need her to paint?"

"That is the question we need to answer." Reaper glanced out the window, seeing nothing but that terrified look in Harmony's eyes. He'd find out.

Or die trying.

CHAPTER 8

Harmony stood in front of the full-length mirror. If she had been wearing this dress for any other reason, it would've been a Cinderella moment. She'd never worn designer clothes. It was never in her budget. She'd heard of some designers, but the name embroidered in the label of this dress was foreign to her. Her shoes made her legs look a mile long. Bernard had arranged for a hairdresser, makeup specialist, and nail artist this afternoon. Her blonde hair was swept to one side and fell in long curls past her shoulder. She didn't recognize her own face. The makeup was flawless. She lifted her fingernails and shook her head. It seemed she always had some Karelian blue or patches of sunshine yellow under her nails. Today, the artificially lengthened nails were painted the exact color of her blue dress. She would've preferred the dress to be longer, but there was no doubt it fit her like a glove. The soft material caressed her skin as she walked. She feared Talib's reaction when he saw her. If his unabated lust had been prominent before, she could only imagine the comments and the leers she would receive tonight.

"Well, my little American ragamuffin does clean up well." Bernard stood in her doorway, dressed in a tux.

"This isn't me. I doubt I'll be able to walk by the end of the night." The four-inch heels were a new experience. She'd worn heels once or twice to dances, but for the most part, she wore tennis shoes.

"It's a good thing you're not doing much walking. You are there to be seen. An asset that needed to be dressed up. Tell me the rules." Bernard slowly walked around her. His eyes were assessing, but not like Talib's. Bernard was looking for flaws, not trying to intimidate her with sexual advances.

"I speak only when in your presence. I stay with either you or Talib. If asked a question, I defer to you or Talib to answer it." As Bernard had stated earlier, she was a prop. Although why they needed to pull her out of the apartment in Paris and parade her around was beyond her. She and that dancing bear in the circus had more in common each day.

"Good. Now, come, we will meet Talib at the venue." Bernard walked to the door and opened it for her.

"Why do I need to be there?" She had asked before, but Bernard had always refused to answer.

Bernard shut the door behind them. "When directed to supply the artist, one does not question the order."

"Who do you work for?" Obviously, if they had been ordered to have her show up, they worked for someone.

Bernard stopped at the elevator and pushed the button. He turned to look at her and lifted an eyebrow. "That information is not for you. That is information that will get you killed. I would hate to lose the best artist I've coached in the last decade."

She scoffed, "Coached? You mean lied to, kidnapped, and blackmailed."

The door opened and she snapped her mouth shut. Bernard escorted her into the elevator and pushed the button to go to the lobby of the hotel. He leaned down and whispered although there was no one else in the car, "You have natural talent, true. But you cannot discount my value in your education."

She snapped her head in his direction. "Education." She stared at him for a moment. "You have educated me. I now know exactly what evil is. I know what hatred is. I know what fear is." And she had a damn good idea of what vengeance entailed. She was an excellent student. One day, she'd surpass her teacher.

Bernard's eyes narrowed as he looked at her. "I do not like the determination I see in your eyes, little one. Do not forget, you will pay with your life and the lives of others if you fail tonight."

"I won't fail." If she could get them to believe she'd never run or never try to escape, they might let down their guard. "I will not have the blood of innocent people on my hands. Unlike you."

"There is no blood on my hands." Bernard gave a low evil chuckle. "Talib's, on the other hand, are bathed in it."

Harmony closed her eyes. She had no doubt that Talib was at the center of many evil things. His evilness radiated off him. Every time he was close to her, she cringed inwardly. It was everything she could do not to run away from the man. But she would stand her ground. She would be strong, and she would find a way out of this.

Bernard whisked her through the foyer and into

a waiting limo. She'd never ridden in such luxury. Her eyes bounced from the tuck and roll leather seats to the small bar, television, and... dear God, that was a telephone. What would she do with access to an unmonitored telephone? That was something she hadn't considered. Who would she call? How could she warn Maggie? Was Maggie being watched? She sat in the corner of the limo as they drove, pondering the questions she needed answers to. There were so many unknowns. She'd bide her time. As long as Talib left her alone, she could afford to wait, watch, and listen.

It was a short drive to the beautiful little chapel. The uplighting on the façade was nothing less than spectacular. She let Bernard take her hand through his arm as they approached the doorway. Another limo drove up as they entered the ancient building. Bernard reached into his suit jacket and presented two gold metal discs the size of a credit card to the guard at the door. The man inserted the discs into a machine. He glanced at Bernard and nodded to the interior door. Another man stepped out of the shadows and opened the door.

The interior of the chapel had been converted into what looked like an artist's studio from the turn of the twentieth century. Roped-off sections held old paints, brushes, half-finished canvases, and other tools of her craft. There were numerous paintings along the wall, all immaculately lit and displayed. However, the Pissarro that she'd copied was standing in the center of the chapel. Two of her other paintings, both masters', were on display beside the Pissarro. Red velvet ropes held the sixty or so spectators at bay. Her stomach fell. They truly were going to auction off her work as originals.

She stopped in her tracks, causing Bernard to glance down at her in frustration.

"The Degas and Renoir are on exhibit at the Louvre."

He gave a distracted look toward the paintings. "Indeed. It is of no concern. There. There is Talib. The man beside him is who you were to be seen by. A tease, as it were. We will make our way there." Bernard kept his hand over the top of hers, forcing her to walk with him.

She looked at the man next to Talib. He was older, perhaps in his 50s. The man had dark brown hair that he had allowed to gray at the temples. The older man seemed to be a larger, older version of Talib. Rich, entitled, and disgusting.

As they neared, a tall, beautiful blonde with ice white hair walked up to the duo. Talib's expression was almost comical. The woman's beauty had poleaxed him. His mouth dropped open and his eyes widened almost as if the shock of seeing her beauty had short-circuited his brain. The blonde was at least six inches taller than Talib even without her high heels. She looked eye to eye at the man Harmony was here to be dangled in front of like a shiny object. The larger man leaned forward and kissed both cheeks of the striking woman. She smiled politely as he introduced her to Talib. Talib took her hand and kissed it. Harmony could see the moment the woman registered Talib's creep factor. Her polite smile fell from her face, and she jerked her hand out of the man's grasp.

The larger man's eyes narrowed, and he turned his attention toward Talib. Unfortunately, that was when Bernard chose to intervene.

"Good evening. I believe we were expected?"

Talib's eyes flashed to them. The sneer at the corner of his lip hitched up. "Indeed. I believe you know Bernard LaVette. This is our associate." Her name wasn't given. Harmony lowered her eyes to the ground. She was there to be seen. Fine. She wasn't allowed to speak; she wouldn't look, either.

A soft, husky female voice said in French, "How do you do? My name is Raquel. It is obvious these so-called gentlemen do not know how to do an introduction."

Harmony lifted her eyes to meet the woman's. She didn't say a word but offered her hand. The woman's eyebrows rose, and she looked from man to man. Bernard offered an explanation, "Our friend does not speak French."

The woman smiled. Harmony recognized the Italian as she spoke. When Harmony didn't respond, the woman spoke in what sounded to be German. Finally, she spoke in English, "How do you do?"

Harmony gave the briefest smile. "I am well, thank you."

The beautiful woman smiled a dazzling display of beautiful teeth. "My name is Raquel. It is very nice to meet you. What is your name?"

Harmony glanced at Bernard, who nodded ever so slightly. "My name is Harmony Flinn." Bernard's hand, which was still covering hers, clamped down. Yes, she'd overstepped, but it was a risk she was willing to take.

"You are an American? Yes?" Raquel quizzed.

"My dear, why don't you go get us some champagne?" the new man that had provided no introduction for himself prompted.

The woman turned to her date, or boyfriend, or

husband, and gave him a look that would melt an iceberg in three seconds. "Are there not waiters?" She looked around and caught the eye of one of the waiters circling and called him over. She then turned to her companion. "I don't wait on anyone." Harmony tacked on a mental first strike for the older man. She didn't see this woman being bossed around by these criminals.

The older man immediately backtracked. His apology was in French, and Harmony understood every third or fourth word, but there was no doubt the man was groveling. The blonde demurred a bit and allowed the man to kiss her cheek. However, the fact that she was extremely put out couldn't be ignored.

She turned to look at Bernard just as he and Talib exchanged glances. Bernard grasped her hand in a painful grip, pressing it against his arm. "We should circulate. Please, excuse us." Harmony winced but allowed herself to be steered away.

That's when she saw Roman.

She froze and gave a small gasp. Terrified, she looked down because looking at him could spark Talib's interest and seal Roman's fate.

"What is the matter?" Bernard hissed at her.

"I… ahh… I twisted my ankle. I told you, I was

not used to walking in high heels." It was the only lie she could think to tell the man. She lifted her eyes just as Roman walked by. He flicked a glance over her and Bernard, but there was no recognition. Nothing. They were dismissed as he made his way toward the Pissarro.

"Walk with me to the corner." Bernard hissed his order.

She used Bernard for support. Her knees were weak and her legs were shaking. The man that had passed by was an older version of the boy she once knew. He carried at least 50 or 60 more pounds of muscle. The suit he wore was immaculately tailored, and every female head in the small chapel turned to watch him stride past. Roman Alexander had changed from the lanky young man she recalled. He was exceptionally handsome.

When they reached the shadowed darkness of the corner, Bernard gripped her hand and squeezed it tightly. She gasped and then bent under the pain. "Stop!" She cried the word in a hushed whisper.

"If your hands were not so valuable, I would break every finger." Bernard squeezed harder.

"What did I do?" She gasped again as he twisted her hand in his tightened grip.

"You know what you did. You could have replied

with your first name only, but you didn't, did you?" Bernard ground the words out between clenched teeth.

"You gave me permission." Harmony winced as the twist of her wrist went a bit further.

"You knew what I expected of you. You will pay for that. Remember your place. Talib will make sure you understand. I tried to warn you," Bernard sneered.

"I don't understand what I did wrong. I introduced myself. You gave me permission to do so." If Talib ever touched her, she'd either kill him or kill herself. "If you want these paintings, keep him away from me." She wrenched her arm away from Bernard, stumbling a bit as she freed herself.

The blonde who had introduced herself earlier walked in their direction. "My new friend! I'm just going to the ladies' room, come with me and we will fix your lipstick, yes?"

"I believe her makeup is perfect." Bernard said the words with an admiration that almost sickened her stomach.

"Because you are not a woman!" Raquel grabbed Harmony's hand and turned back to Bernard, smiling. "We are just going to powder our noses. I will bring her back alive and well. How much trouble can either of us get into in front of a mirror?" She ran a manicured fingertip around Bernard's collar and straightened his bowtie.

Bernard turned and glared at Harmony, but his tone, which was all the woman could hear with his head turned as it was, was indulging. "One never knows, my dear." He narrowed his eyes in a warning and stepped out of the way.

Raquel laughed as if he had told the most remarkable joke. She led Harmony into the small powder room. Raquel held a finger up to her mouth while she carried on a stream of conversation about a shopping trip early this week. Nothing the woman said required an answer.

Harmony watched as the statuesque woman pulled out a small, clear... hearing aid? The blonde pulled back her hair and tapped her ear. Harmony took the tiny device and inserted it, hiding it under the fall of curls Bernard's hairdresser had styled this afternoon. The woman took out a bottle of perfume and squirted it on Harmony's wrists, all while talking a mile a minute. She sat her purse down after putting the perfume back into the beautiful clutch. She didn't stop talking about a dress she'd seen. She turned to Harmony and held up a small piece of paper.

"Is your life in danger tonight?"

Harmony shook her head. She didn't think so. They wanted more paintings. Raquel nodded, still talking about the material that was fabulous to the touch. Another square and she scribbled, *"We can hear when you talk. Keep it in your ear."*

Harmony nodded. The woman turned on the water and held the squares under the tap. They dissolved instantly. She handed Harmony a lipstick and turned toward the mirror to apply her own, still talking.

Without warning, the door opened and Talib stepped in.

Raquel stood up straight and spit a torrent of French words at the man. Outraged, she stomped off and pushed Talib out of the way, opening the door.

Harmony stared at the man as he approached her. "Don't touch me."

"Actions have repercussions." Talib grabbed her by the neck and used both thumbs to exert pressure at the hollow of her throat. She struggled and gasped, scratching at his hands. White blotches formed in front of her eyes before he relented and released his hold. "Step out of line again and there will be more than a mild reminder. Do you think you are irreplaceable? You are alive because I owe a small debt, never forget that." Talib smiled at her before he lifted her chin and licked her neck, leaving a trail of saliva on her skin.

She sank down to the small, cushioned chair and gasped for air. If they could hear everything, they heard what had happened. Whoever "they" were. She drew deeper and deeper pulls of air before she heard hushed arguing outside the door. She stood up, made sure her legs could hold her, and walked out of the small powder room. The tall blonde had obviously told her sugar daddy what had transpired because that man was speaking in hushed, rushed words, none of which she could hear.

Bernard spoke from behind her. "You have no idea how hard it will be to keep him from your door now. Do behave. He still owes me, and I want those paintings."

She turned and looked at him, her voice raspy after Talib had nearly choked her to death. "What do you mean?"

There was an announcement from the front of the chapel. She got two words, auction and commence. Bernard pulled her toward the front of the chapel and her imitation of the Pissarro. They moved closer but stayed somewhat behind the crowd. Harmony couldn't focus on what was happening, trying to look for Roman without Bernard figuring out what she was doing. That man had to be Roman. *He had to be.* She reached up and made sure the tiny clear earpiece was still in her ear and glanced to her right. He wasn't there. She scanned the crowd casually and slowly made her way back to the man she thought was Roman. Her heart sank. He was next to Talib, and they were quietly laughing. The man she thought was Roman leaned down and whispered something else. Talib clasped him on the shoulder and nodded vigorously. They exchanged a handshake before Roman strolled away.

She forced herself to look at her paintings. There were a series of men in small groups at the front of the room and she tried to understand what was happening. It appeared as though they were bidding against each other with a numbered paddle they'd been provided for the smaller paintings.

When the Pissarro came up for auction, there were three groups that bid against each other. She watched as one of the men who held a paddle shook his head sharply when the auctioneer pointed to him. He and four other men exited the chapel immediately. The bidding went on, punctuated by moments of silence as the two remaining camps conferred. Finally, both held up their paddles and the auctioneer slammed the hammer down. "Sold for one hundred and fifty million Euros."

Her gasp couldn't have been heard amongst the reserved applause of the remaining crowd. She turned her astounded stare to Bernard.

"As I said, we will be using your talents for the rest of your life, however long that may be. Behave and it may be longer."

As they turned to leave, Bernard ran into the man she could have sworn was Roman. Bernard bounced backward and excused his clumsiness. The man brushed off his tux jacket and spoke in perfect French, "Not a problem. Excuse me."

That voice. No matter what language it was, she'd recognize that voice. She stared up at him, and he nodded at her without an ounce of recognition in his expression.

Bernard winced and rubbed his arm, glancing at the man she thought was Roman.

"What's wrong?"

"Nothing, just a sharp discomfort."

She wished it had been a heart attack. Instead, she stumbled forward when Bernard tugged on her. "Are we leaving?"

"You've made your appearance. I asked Talib not

to leave a mark. There is notable bruising developing around your throat."

Bernard's comment suggested it was her fault that she was bruising. "Sorry, the next time he tries to choke me, I'll have the decency not to bruise," she grumbled as they stepped out of the chapel.

"If he wanted you dead, this conversation wouldn't be happening." Bernard shoved her none too gently into the limo. She scrambled across the seat and wedged herself into the corner. She fluffed her hair and checked her little earpiece without drawing attention to the act. It was still there. She turned and looked out the window as they drove back to the hotel. She prayed the people the woman worked for could hear her. She wished they could talk to her, tell her who they were, and let her know that she'd be okay. She sighed. *If wishes were fishes, we'd all be fed*. Again, her aunt's voice echoed through her mind. Yeah, she was serving up a banquet with all the wishes she'd been making.

CHAPTER 9

The overwhelming desire to slice Talib's neck and let him bleed out until he was dead ate at Reaper. The gnawing need to make the motherfucker pay for what he'd done to Harmony had to be shoved down and caged. The mission required it. He stood beside Talib and talked about art. Along with his invitation, he received background on Pissarro, his paintings, and the legendary fifth self-portrait.

"Are you interested in hard-to-obtain art?" Talib asked him after he'd introduced himself.

"The harder to obtain the more worthwhile, don't you agree?" He smiled at the man. It took every ounce of skill he'd ever acquired.

"Oh, absolutely. I haven't seen you at the recent auctions. Are you here with one of the contingents?"

Talib gave him the once over and then returned his gaze to the Pissarro, Degas, and Renoir.

"Contingent? No, I'm here alone, and until recently, my interests were more in the way of... living art forms. Women are extraordinary examples of the beauty of art." He gave a self-deprecating chuckle. "There are many different ways to enjoy that aesthetic, wouldn't you agree?"

Talib shot him a sideways glance. "I would, but my interests in living art are a bit on the darker side."

"Only a bit? Shame, the darker the better as far as I'm concerned." He shrugged. He wanted to vomit. He knew what Talib was into. That information was also included in his briefing. The son of a bitch had a fetish, and although there was suspicion, according to the documentation, no one could prove Behar had actually killed any of the women he had abused. Reaper didn't honestly care if it could be proven. Safe, sane, and consensual, he got. What Talib apparently did to females was sadistic in the extreme.

Talib chuckled and motioned for Reaper to lean down. When he obliged, the man nodded in Val's direction. "That one. I'd like to take that one home and make her beg over and over again."

Reaper laughed at the man's words. He laughed because he knew as soon as the door closed Val wouldn't be the one who was begging. Talib's ambitions were way out of his league, and he was no match for that assassin.

The auctioneer announced the beginning of the bidding. Reaper continued to talk to Talib in low tones as the crowd gathered around the paintings. He removed a pair of glasses from his tux jacket, placing them on his face. Reaper turned on the hidden camera in the frames. Scanning the crowd slowly, he tried to get a solid profile or full-face shot of each person bidding. There had to be a connection between the art that was being auctioned and the primary targets on which they were gathering information.

As the bidding continued, he watched paddles rise and fall and recorded the entire process via his glasses. The auctioneer merely noted the paddle number, not indicating a winning bid. Reaper studied the auctioneer and the crowd. As bidders pulled out of the auction and turned in their paddles, they were given a tablet. Unfortunately, he wasn't close enough to see what information they were inputting. He scanned each face as they bid, left, or remained to bid again.

The auctioneer moved on to the Pissarro. Reaper stared at the painting. Based on the brief he'd read prior to coming tonight, the highest estimates of what the painting would sell for couldn't touch the astronomical amount paid tonight.

He saw Harmony and moved in her direction. Val had taken her into the powder room. He wasn't sure what the assassin was up to, but there had been a reason. When he noticed her and her jailer-slash-escort start to move, he stepped into the man. With practiced ease, he marked his prey. Nanotechnology enabled him to plant a mini-RF transmitter on the man with a small jab of a tiny needle. The chip couldn't be detected by a nonprofessional. Not reacting to Harmony during the process nearly gutted him.

As he stood outside and waited for his car to pick him up, he watched Val and her primary walkout. She had the man groveling at her feet. He had seen it from across the room. He wouldn't question the assassin's methods.

As if Val was a dangling, shiny object, Talib bit the killer's baited hook. Guardian would engineer another run-in with the man for him. One thing he knew for a fact after a short amount of time in the man's presence this evening: Talib was full of himself and wanted everyone to be in awe of him. Maybe it had something to do with having one of the richest men in the world as your father. Reaper certainly didn't care about the root cause of the bastard's needy existence. However, he would ingratiate himself and find out exactly what Talib knew. One way or the other, the man was going to tell him. Personally, he'd prefer torturing the information out of the bastard. Although that method of killing was Phoenix's specialty, he'd witnessed his friend work a time or two and was a fast learner.

His phone vibrated in his pocket. He waited until he was seated in his chauffeur-driven limo and traveling back to his resort before he pulled it out of his pocket.

>*She has an earpiece.*

He looked at Val's text and narrowed his eyes as he typed his response.

>*Why?*

>*So, you can talk to her. Find out what is going on. I'll get a replacement.*

>*Not in the game plan.*

>*I don't like games.*

>*Thank you.*

She knew what he needed even if he'd never admit it. He needed to talk to Harmony. To make sure she was okay.

>*What are friends for?*

Reaper smiled at Val's text and pocketed his phone, wishing the driver was going faster. His earpiece was back in the room. Obviously, Val had planned on giving her earpiece to Harmony all along. A smile tugged at his lips. He could program the earpieces so only the two of them were in the conversation. All it took was a couple of commands from his phone. Guardian's technology was going to enable him to talk to Harmony for the first time in over ten years.

After checking all his countermeasures to ensure his room hadn't been entered, he stripped off his jacket, removed his bowtie, and loosened his tuxedo shirt from his slacks. Reaper palmed his phone, called up the necessary app, and initiated a secure link between the two earpieces. He inserted his earpiece and listened. There was little that he could discern. Perhaps a faraway television show? He drew a steadying breath and released it before he spoke, "Harmony, can you hear me?"

"Holy shit!" Her shout nearly deafened him. He hit the control to lower his volume.

"What is the problem?" Bernard's voice yelled from the distance.

"Tell him you saw a spider."

"Ah, I thought I saw a spider..." Her voice was shaking.

"Step on it."

"No shit, Sherlock," Harmony mumbled.

Reaper waited for a moment before he asked, "Did he buy it?"

"Yes, I think so. Roman?" She whispered the words. "Oh, God, tell me I'm not imagining this. Please. Tell me that was you tonight." Her voice rose as she spoke. It held a tinge of hysteria.

"Don't say another word. When you can do so without raising any suspicion, go into the bathroom and turn on the taps. Whisper, I can hear you." He heard her move and a door shut behind her, then heard the shower turn on.

"Okay." She whispered the word again and he adjusted the gain to block out some of the background noise.

"First, some questions. Are you safe?"

"As long as I keep painting, yes. If I stop, they threatened Maggie and you."

"What about that bastard Talib?" If he was hurting her, he'd have to kill the man.

"He choked me tonight as punishment. I said too much," she hissed. "The bruising is pretty bad."

The growl that came from him was unbidden and

unpreventable. He swallowed the words he wanted to say. Instead, he got down to business. "You can leave the earpiece in at all times. As long as it is lodged in your ear, we have a way to track you. We can talk to you and you to us. Right now, the two of us are the only ones on the channel. After our conversation tonight there will be someone monitoring you at all times. The people I work for are trying to gather information about the connection between the forged artwork and other situations we're investigating. Can you tell me about what happened to you?"

"I'm not the first one they duped. I'm the first that they kept, I think. They had several students who did one or two paintings for them but weren't good at mimicking the masters. Come get me, please? I didn't know they'd sell my work. I swear."

"I know, sweetheart. I know." He closed his eyes as the term of endearment fell from his lips. "Do you know of any other auctions that are planned?"

"I heard Talib and Bernard talking about something in Paris in a month's time. They've been pushing me to finish another work."

"What hotel are you at now and what is your address in Paris?"

She told him but added, "They said I'm being

watched. My phone back in Paris is monitored, that's how they found out about you. Maggie told me you'd been back. I don't know if they can see inside my apartment."

"We'll take a look at that." He wanted to do the recon himself. If they had electronics on her, disabling them wouldn't be a problem. Surveillance? He'd find the bastards in a heartbeat.

"Who do you work for? Why can't you take me out of here now?" Desperation tinged her voice again.

"Because, sweetheart, you are smack dab in the middle of some epic-level international issues. Think James Bond on steroids."

"Are you James or one of the weird-named villains?"

"They call me Alexander, Roman Alexander." He mimicked his favorite actor's Scottish accent.

He leaned forward when he heard a loud knock and a man's voice, distorted but clear enough to understand, barked, "What are you doing in there?"

"Taking a crap, you bastard!" Harmony yelled the words.

"Disgusting American."

"Disgusting but effective." She whispered the

words to him as she flushed the toilet. "I need to get in the shower, or he'll know something's off."

"Go ahead, the earpiece is waterproof."

"Wait, you can't see me, right?"

He chuckled. "No." *Although I've thought about you just about every night for the last ten years.* "You've matured into a beautiful woman. Besides, I've seen you naked before." He teased her a little bit to help her with her nerves.

He could hear material rustling. "Yeah, well, that was ten years ago. It would be embarrassing and awkward now. I was dressed up like a doll tonight. This isn't me. This isn't anything close to me."

"I know. If you had a choice, you'd be wearing jeans, a t-shirt, and Chucks." He leaned forward and stared out the dark window. "I've kept track of you." The sound of the water now was much louder.

"I know. The paints. It was you, right?"

"It was." He closed his eyes.

"Yeah, well… thank you for that. Thanks." She choked up at the end of that statement but held it together.

He whispered, "I've missed you so damn bad."

"But not bad enough to come whisk me away in the middle of the night."

There it was. Harmony was hurt and maybe a

little pissed. He understood where the feelings were coming from. "Life wasn't easy for me for many years."

He trained like a maniac and worked from the time he got up to the time he dropped exhausted into bed. Sometimes, falling into bed was days after he'd started. He threw everything he had into paying back the company that saved his ass.

"Do you think it was easy for me?" She whispered the words, and he heard the shower door open and then the flap of material as she dried off.

"I know it wasn't."

"Hold on." She turned off the shower and then turned on the water in the tap. "I'm not mad at you. You did what you had to do. It's just... I wish I'd gone with you. Things got hard after my aunt and uncle died."

"I know." He could only imagine what a prick Delbert was to her. He had to change the subject; they were running out of time. "When do you leave for Paris?"

"They don't tell me anything. I'm not sure."

"Then we'll listen in. I'll patch through and talk with you tomorrow night."

"How will I know that it's okay to talk when I get home?"

"Someone will go through your apartment and make sure it is safe." He'd guarantee it.

"How long, Roman? How long until I'm out of this hell?"

"Let me work with my superiors on that, and when we talk, I'll have an answer." At least he hoped to have one.

"Roman?"

"Yes?"

"I've missed you so damn much." She cut off the water.

"No more than I've missed you. Go to sleep. Soon, this nightmare will be over. We'll talk again tomorrow."

He opened his phone and tapped the necessary icons to have the audio recorded and transcribed for Val's earpiece. It would send up red flags. He closed the app and glanced at his watch. *Maybe two minutes? Less, probably.* The phone rang and he chuckled. "Sunset Operative Fourteen."

"Stand by for the Annex."

"Annex on."

"Operator Two-Seven-Four clear."

"Explain the tracker on Valkyrie. Is she under duress?"

"It isn't on her. She gave her earpiece to

Harmony."

There was a prolonged silence on the other end of the line. "Interesting thought process." Anubis sighed. "I'll requisition another for her. It should be there before you both leave."

"I don't know when my primary is traveling back to Paris. I made contact and established a report based on the preferences in the information provided. I'll need to know where to run into him again. Preferably soon."

"We can work that. Did you get an address as to where they are staying?"

"I did." He rattled off the hotel name and her room number.

"I'll text you the checkout date that the hotel has in their computer system. Were you able to tag either of them?"

"Both. Talib when I was speaking with him and Bernard when they were leaving, but Harmony's earpiece should give us a location of Bernard while they're in Cannes. I believe he's her keeper on this trip. Harmony thinks her apartment in Paris is being watched. I'm unsure as to the accuracy of that information."

"Affirmative. I'll have someone inspect the apartment after ensuring there is no one watching." He could hear Anubis typing in the background.

"Check for human surveillance once they get back, too. Any information on the pictures from the auction?"

"Yeah, that's a given, she'll get the full nine yards. We want to know who has eyes on her. The pictures? I haven't been briefed on anything on the pictures as of yet. Archangel has a standing sitrep with us, you're now on the call participant log. The request for monitoring the earpiece was just approved. You did let her know we'd be listening? To everything?"

"She knows. I think it helps. She's terrified. They are using Maggie and Roman Alexander as leverage. That, and Talib has threatened her. He choked her tonight for overstepping her boundaries."

"Can I kill the bastards?" Anubis asked.

"The line forms behind me." If they weren't targeted, he'd leave them wishing they were dead.

"Undoubtedly. How did the reunion go? Mess with your head?"

Reaper understood the reason for the question. His handler needed to know where he was mentally. "A bit. It's been ten years. She knew why I left; hell, she told me to leave, but she had a hard life and then she fell into this pit of vipers. She wants out. I can't blame her." She deserved to be happy and to be free from controlling fuckers like Delbert, Bernard, and Talib.

"You'll still be able to work the primary?"

"Without a problem. Talib loves to talk about Talib. I'll stroke the man's ego. Val had both men eating out of her palm. Talib wants what Ardan thinks he has."

Anubis mused, "Working both ends against the middle?"

"She's either playing games or has a brilliant idea. Baby Behar gets in trouble with Ardan, and Daddy Behar shows up to put junior in his place."

"Or he puts Ardan in his place," Anubis countered. "Blood is thicker than water."

Reaper shook his head. "Money speaks louder. My bet is Baby Behar gets slapped or called home to be spanked."

"I'll take that bet." Anubis chuckled. "The call with Archangel is in a couple hours. Get some rest."

He disconnected the call and dropped his phone. Fuck, hearing her voice tonight was unexpected, and God… it *was* a mind fuck. He kicked off his shoes and stripped out of the tux. He headed into the bathroom and started his shower, stepping in almost immediately. The cold water did nothing to diminish the feelings her voice had catapulted to the forefront of his mind.

Harmony was his first lover. He dipped his head under the water and thought about how they'd fumbled their way through discovering how to please each other. Hell, the first time they made love he was seventeen and she was fifteen. It sucked. He knew he hurt her, and when that happened, he lost his hard-on. They didn't try again for two months; that wasn't much better, but with time, they found pleasure in each other's bodies. He'd had sex with other women in the last ten years, but that was all it was. Sex. With Harmony, he had history, a story that went back to that day in the trees between the farms. She was such a tough thing, trying not to let that bastard Delbert get the better of her. There was rarely a day that they didn't see each other or at least talk. They'd built intricate plans for the future; he was going to be a police officer and she was going to have her own little shop to sell her paintings. Harmony wanted one of the small houses in town and had decided he was putting a white picket fence around the front yard to keep the dog out of the street.

She'd changed yet hadn't. Her hair was much

longer, and her body had curves that enhanced her figure. The makeup tonight was spectacular, but he preferred to see the freckles that trailed across her nose. Her dark brown lashes didn't need mascara, and her big hazel eyes sparkled without the colored crap on her eyelids. Harmony Flinn was beautiful on the inside and out. She was the measurement standard to which he compared other women. None met the mark she'd placed on his heart or the need her absence had drilled into his soul.

He reached for the French milled soap and rubbed it over his chest. That voice in his ear and the sight of her in that blue dress tonight wouldn't be denied. He'd fantasized about him and Harmony so often; it didn't take long for his body to respond. Only tonight, he was thinking about the woman, not the girl. Cupping his shaft, he braced one arm against the tile wall. Recalling the way her legs looked in those heels and the curve of her ass and rise of her breasts was easy. Without any cognizant direction, his brain had chiseled his memories of her tonight into stone. He ran his palm up and down his shaft, stopping to twist a bit at the head of his cock before he retraced his movement and started again.

As his thoughts drifted to memories of them making love, the feel of her hot core and the memory of her hands traveling down his back, gripping his ass, and begging for him to go deeper and faster sped his slick hand up and down his shaft. The one thing he absolutely craved was to feel her teeth bite into his skin. Harmony was loud when they made love, and to keep quiet, she'd bite his shoulder or neck and seal against his skin as she cried out when she climaxed. Her body would ripple around his cock in rhythmic contractions, and it always drove him over the top. His body spasmed and painted the tile in front of him. He groaned through his climax. Just the thought of being with her again, touching that skin and tasting her lips, crashed his orgasm through his body. He caught his breath and pushed off the wall, standing weak-kneed under the warm water.

He didn't know how, but Harmony and he were not going to be separated again. He grabbed the shampoo as he tried to wrap his head around how that would happen. He could see it now. *I love you and want to marry you, but... well, hey, I'm an assassin. No, you don't need to be shocked or worried about it, I only kill really bad guys... for my country... but not* inside *my country.*

Dear God, he was fucked. He had enough money to leave Guardian, but there was still more he felt called to do for Guardian and his country. He didn't rent out his skills to the highest bidder. His was a solemn duty for his country and for the people who couldn't protect themselves. If any of the monsters he'd eliminated had been allowed to live, thousands upon thousands of people would have died. It wasn't his opinion. He'd seen the evidence; he'd witnessed the atrocities, and he had no doubt the bastards would continue to rain hell down upon the earth. How could he ask Harmony to be a part of his world? Cranking off the water, his mind immediately punched back with, *'How could you not? You'll lose her again, this time for good.'* He toweled off and dropped into the bed. No, that wasn't an option. He sighed and thumped his pillow. *It never really was an option, was it? You've never gotten over her.* He closed his eyes and sighed. He couldn't deny the truth. He still loved her and wouldn't leave her again. He'd figure out a way to make it work. Somehow.

CHAPTER 10

Harmony stood at the window and stared out at the powder-white beaches of southern France. The sun was shining brightly and there were a vast number of sun worshippers lying out on colorful towels or resort-provided chairs. She'd barely slept last night and the dark circles under her eyes bore testament to that fact.

"It is beautiful, is it not?" Bernard spoke from behind her. She didn't bother to answer. "Would you like to go to the beach?"

She blinked and looked at him. That was a stupid question; of course, she wanted to go to the beach, but she also knew they'd never trust her. And the bruising around her throat would draw attention that they wouldn't want.

Bernard shrugged. "Perhaps someday, once we know we can trust you." He mused the same words she'd thought a second before. "We're flying home today. Talib will follow in a few days' time." He pointed to a blue print silk scarf that he'd obviously placed on the bed. "Wear that around your neck. No one is to see Talib's punishment. Understood?"

She grabbed the scarf and worked it through itself, making a casual drape that covered her neck. The jeans and white shirt she was wearing would work with the color of the scarf.

"Pack. We leave in five minutes."

She pulled the case out of the small closet as she asked, "Why isn't Talib coming with us?"

"He has matters to attend to."

"Concerning the auction?" She pulled the dresses they'd bought for her from the hangers and shoved them into the case, not bothering to fold them. Yeah, they were expensive, but unless they forced her to wear them, she wasn't going to do it. Minor acts of rebellion that Talib wouldn't be allowed to punish her for were now her focus.

Bernard walked back to the common door that separated their rooms. "Why do you ask?"

She stood up and snorted. "I'm hoping the bastard will be here for longer than a couple of days."

Bernard lifted an eyebrow. "Don't think that there isn't anyone to keep you in line when he's gone."

She walked over to the dresser and scooped out the clothes she'd been told to put in them but hadn't worn. "I have no doubt you have a backup asshole that will come rough me up if I get out of line."

Bernard walked over to her and put a finger under her chin and lifted it so she was forced to look up at him. "You fail to understand, my dear. You are necessary, but you aren't the only one we can leverage. You happen to be convenient *and* talented. Remain convenient and you'll stay alive. Don't bite the hand that feeds you, or you will be put down."

She jerked her chin from his hold. "Keep that bastard away from me and I'll be convenient."

"You make good on your end, and I will see what can be done to have Talib control himself. After all, he does owe me."

"The van Gogh I'm painting needs to be done by the end of the month, correct?"

"It does." Bernard leaned against the wall. "Why do you ask this now?"

"Because it's difficult and I'll need to immerse myself in the project to make it perfect and get it done in time."

Bernard cocked his head. "And?"

"And Talib is a disturbance to my ability to work. Perhaps you make sure he is removed first, and I will show you how compliant to your directions I can be. My specialty is the Impressionist era, van Gogh is post-Impressionist. I need to be able to concentrate." She pushed the clothes down and zipped the lid of her suitcase shut.

Bernard stared at her with narrowed eyes. "You will be watched. If you step out of line, even a paintbrush hair's width out, Talib won't be stopped."

"I may be hardheaded, but I'm not stupid. Call off your dog and I'll paint my fingers off. Oh, and change the lock on my door so he can't let himself in anymore."

Bernard lifted an eyebrow. "We have a deal."

She slid the suitcase to the floor and extended the handle. "And I'm ready to go."

Bernard nodded to his room. She pulled the case after her. He called for an attendant to retrieve their bags and offered her a seat at his breakfast table. "Are you hungry?"

"No, thank you." She was, but she'd eat when she got home. She prayed the people Roman were working with had been listening. He said they would be, so he'd know she was flying back to Paris today.

Would he stay here or follow her? She had no idea what to expect. The boy she knew wasn't the same as the man that she'd talked to last night. This version of Roman was a puzzle. He wore clothes that cost more than ten acres of land back home. He spoke French fluently. *Right?* Yes, he had to know the language. He'd apologized to Bernard for running into him in French. He was shocked to see her in Cannes, but not at seeing her at the auction. The woman, that absolutely beautiful woman, worked with him. She closed her eyes and rested her head against the wall as they waited for the attendant to come get the bags. Roman was absolutely drop-dead gorgeous and so was that woman. Her eyes popped open. Was Roman married or involved with some-one? He'd said he'd thought of her over the last ten years, but... what if he'd found someone and moved on?

Glancing at Bernard to make sure he was occu-pied, which he was, busily typing on his phone, she dropped her head into her hands and rubbed her face. Damn it. Why hadn't she thought of that? She'd ask him the next time they spoke. If they spoke. Hell, if it wasn't for the little piece of clear plastic in her ear, last night could have been a dream—except it wasn't. Her hand went to her neck. She'd seen the look in Talib's eyes. He got off on choking her. But this was more than that. He wanted to kill her. He didn't need to speak the words; the piercing gaze laced with lust and excitement said more than his words could ever articulate.

A soft knock at the door put them in motion. She followed Bernard to the car, through the airport, and onto the plane. The flight was short, and they soon landed in Paris. A car whisked them back to the city center. Bernard escorted her to her apartment. "The painting is a priority, as you said. Food will be delivered Mondays and Thursdays. You have a number to reach me if you need any personal items that are not provided by the delivery service. Your phone is monitored, and you are being watched. Step outside this apartment or call for help and you will meet Talib again. This time, he will not be so gentle."

Bernard spun and walked down the stairs. She shut the door, locked it, and then put the small chain across the door.

"There is someone watching the front of the building. As of yet, no one is monitoring the rear of the building."

Harmony jumped, shouting, "Holy shit!"

"Sorry, you're not used to the comms device yet, are you?" a disembodied female voice asked.

"Oh, God, oh, man, you almost stroked me out. Shit, you guys have got to stop doing that." She grabbed at her chest and fell back against the door.

"Again, sorry about that, but as I was saying, there is a person monitoring the front of your building. Not the back."

"That's because the back door is painted shut. This place should be condemned."

"Do you have access to a fire escape?"

"If I break a window, yeah. Who is this?"

"A friend," the voice avoided answering her. "We checked for cameras and electronic listening devices. We didn't find any. With that asshat's last warning, we'll check neighboring apartments to see if they harbor any personnel that may be monitoring you."

"You can do that?" Harmony slid down the door and landed on her butt.

"I can have it done. It would be a couple days before I could be in Paris."

"Yeah, okay. So, what's next?" She wiped the sweat off her brow. Man, the chick gave her a scare.

"You go about your daily life. If you need me, I'll be here monitoring you."

"All day, every day?"

The voice laughed. "Yes."

"Are you like a robot or something?" She stared up at the plaster ceiling of her apartment. Prison. Whatever.

"No, completely human, I assure you. You can call me the operator."

"Right… operator as in 'hold please' or operator as in 'James Bond sneak around in the dark and kill shit' type of operator?"

The laugh in her ear made her smile. "A bit of both, but way more of the first. Again, I'm sorry to have startled you. If you need anything, just talk. We'll hear you."

"We'll?"

"A figure of speech. Are you going to be okay?"

She glanced up at the small chain that locked Talib out. "For now. Did you hear this morning?"

"Yes. Good negotiation on your part."

"Lord, it wasn't negotiation, it was desperation," she half-whispered.

"Just remember, you aren't alone any longer."

She pushed off the floor and grabbed the handle of her suitcase. "Tell me something, operator. If Talib kicked down my door right now, how long would it take someone to get here?"

"I'm sorry, I'm not authorized to disclose that information." The woman did sound a bit put out about it, which didn't help but did make her feel a little less alone.

"I've got to get to work. If I don't finish this painting in time, we may have to test how fast you can get here." She wheeled her new suitcase into the corner of her tiny bedroom and left it there.

"I'm here but going silent."

"Okay, thanks. Oh, and please, don't talk to me when I'm working. I could only imagine what that brushstroke would look like."

"I'll pass that along." The operator chuckled. "We are silent but listening."

Harmony grabbed her oversized smock and headed to the studio. Escaping into her art, even if it was copying someone else's work, gave her the ability to focus on details, centimeter by centimeter, blocking everything else out.

Reaper eased out of the limo and gazed at the large white stucco building. The brass plaque at the door simply read, "Established 1859." In French, of course. He knocked on the door as his limo pulled away. A butler in full livery answered the door and produced a silver tray. As instructed, Reaper placed a jade and gold chip that he'd been provided earlier this morning onto the tray.

"This way, sir." The man made a gesture, and Reaper followed. A mental smile ticked as a huge bouncer shut the door behind the butler. A good sign for the safety of the ladies who worked in this brothel. He followed the butler into an elegantly appointed fifteen-by-fifteen-foot room that was obviously used to screen new clients. "Madam will be with you shortly. May I get you a drink?"

"No, thank you. I prefer not to be encumbered." He watched the little man bow and then waddle out of the room, closing the door behind him. He had no doubt that he was being watched, so he undid the button on his suit jacket and sat down.

There had been no morning status call with Archangel. According to Anubis, it was due to a scheduling conflict. However, Anubis did let him know that Talib would be at this gentleman's club and when. He'd endure the mandatory interview and hopefully take his time watching the activities of the brothel as his afternoon's entertainment. Reinforcing the budding *'friendship'* with the bastard was mandatory if he was to get close to the sick son of a bitch.

A woman entered, and he stood. She opened her

robe, revealing very little in the way of clothes, and placed her hand on her hip. "Welcome, Mr. Belmonte. You come to us highly recommended."

He inclined his chin. "I'm sure."

She pointed to the chair and sat opposite of him after he'd taken a seat. "What do you prefer in your entertainment?"

"I suppose that all depends on the day. Some days call for a distraction, on others, I'd like to work out my frustrations."

"Limits?"

"For me? None." He shrugged, "However, I will adhere to house rules."

"Good. House rules are simple. You may not kill or permanently mark the entertainment or injure them so they cannot be used again. Other than that, we are a full-service establishment."

"I can manage within those limits." He stood. "Where do I see the menu?" He extended his hand to help the woman out of her chair.

"You'll be in the library. Gentlemen of your discerning taste prefer the entertainment we stock there. If the library is not to your tastes, please, ask any of the attendants for management and we will assist you with a more desirable situation. Once you make a selection, you will be afforded a room that is not monitored in any way; however, your entertainment will be checked to ensure all is in working order prior to you leaving."

"But of course." He opened the door, and the woman pointed to her left. He wrapped her hand around his bicep as they strolled down the travertine-tiled hall. She motioned to a door on his left.

"Enjoy your day, Mr. Belmonte. We look forward to serving your needs."

He leered at her and raked her scantily clothed body with his eyes. "Are you ever on the menu?"

She laughed and shook her head, her dark brown hair moving at her shoulders. "I reserve myself for the most discerning palates. People who have a taste for excellence and can afford to pay."

"Which should be every man in this place, no?" He bent over her hand and kissed it.

"It should be, but you'd be surprised." She smiled and withdrew her hand. "Perhaps another day, Mr. Belmonte?"

"I look forward to it." He watched her walk all the way down the hall and turn out of sight before he opened the library door. Soft music was playing, and there were several men sitting in wide wingback chairs. One man had a naked woman on her knees in front of him and he was shoving his cock down her throat. Reaper forced himself to walk to the bar as if the scene was nothing new. The woman's gags and choking drew laughter from the men standing around the bastard that was choking her.

"What can I get you?"

"Water. In a bottle." He looked at the bartender. Her nipples were pierced, and a chain ran between the piercings. Another chain around her neck was linked to the chain between her breasts. Every time she moved, the chains tightened and tugged at her breasts. He waited for his water and stared at the woman. She kept her eyes lowered, but he caught a glimpse of her blown pupils. *Drugged.*

He opened his water and took a drink as three women were brought into the room. Each was handcuffed and shackled. One wore a full head covering without a mouth but had two small holes for her to breathe through her nose. The second wore nipple clamps and a blindfold, the third was pierced and chained like the bartender but wore a box on her head. A tube ran out of the neck hole to a tank of oxygen. He'd seen a similar contraption in a torture film he watched during training. The lining of the box prevented her from hearing, seeing, or breathing. Her life dangled with that bottle of oxygen.

Two of the men who were watching the bastard force his dick down the woman's throat peeled away. One smacked the other on the arm and pointed to the one wearing the isolation box. The man nodded and adjusted himself. "I want her. How much oxygen?"

"One hour, sir, you must return her in fifty-five minutes," the man leading the women replied.

"I'll take the one with the clamps. I'll need heavier ones." The man unhooked the women and gave each man a leash.

"They are provided in the rooms in the wall units," the handler replied as his customers snapped on the leather leashes and tugged the women out of the room. The last woman was taken to the corner, pushed back against the wall for support, and left there. As soon as the women's handler left, one of the men in the library went over to the corner, turned her around, and bent her over. He used his hand and spanked her in loud, ugly cracks. Only the slightest muffled sounds could be heard from the woman.

Reaper's gut rolled. This wasn't safe, sane, or consensual. This was disgusting. Every nerve in his body demanded he act to help the women who were being abused. Every fucking cell. He ground his teeth together and stared hard at each of the men in this room. He'd be able to recall each of their faces. He'd never freelanced before, but now, he was damn sure tempted.

That one; he'd snap his neck and then slam that fucker's head to the table, puncturing his nose through his brain. The bastard still shoving his cock down that woman's throat? He'd show him what it was like to suffocate.

The door to the library opened and Talib walked in. A smile split his face as his eyes went straight to the man beating the woman in the corner. "Harder, Phillipe, she's not even bruising yet."

"She will, Talib, she will." The man picked up a nylon crop and smacked her ass with it, leaving a dark stripe.

"Ah, it is Conrad, right?" Talib bellied up to the bar.

"It is. Funny seeing you here. Talib, correct?"

"That is correct. And no, it shouldn't be a surprise, this is the best game in town." Talib bent over and tugged viciously at the bartender's chain. "You know what I want."

The woman didn't falter although it looked like Talib had pulled hard enough for the piercing to bleed. She walked over to the Scotches and poured the bastard a triple from a very expensive bottle.

"Have you seen anything you like?" Talib waved the glass at the room. "More stock will be arriving soon."

"I've seen a couple items that interested me. Today, I'm window shopping. I have an appointment I must be leaving for, but next time, I'll have time to play."

"You never did tell me the other night. What do you do, Mr. Belmonte?"

He chuckled. The bastard knew exactly what he did; there had been several background checks completed on his current identity. "I don't exactly *do* anything. My father was business partners with David Xavier's father back in the day. My meetings now are to transfer funds from one account to the other and to find my next thrill. And you?"

"Ah, well, my father is also rich, yet I am not my father. So, I jump through work."

He took a drink of his water. "What kind of work?"

Talib took a hefty swig of his liquor. "Arrange things like last night's event. Nothing overly tasking but a bother, nonetheless."

"Ah, I see. I would have loved to purchase that

painting last night. The bidding went through the roof quickly."

Talib slammed his glass back down on the bar and another drink was waiting for him. "Even if you were as rich as David Xavier, you couldn't have won that auction. It wasn't intended for you."

"Probably not. But I'd love to get a painting for a toy. She's... how do I say this politely?"

"Why be polite, here of all places?"

He laughed and lifted his water bottle in a salute. "She's suffered many years while chained in my dungeon. Perhaps the painting will give her respite during my absences."

"You are too nice. Why let them rest? I want them to fear me. I want to see it in their eyes when they know I could kill them. That euphoria of being the one to hold their life in my hands. That's when I explode. It is otherworldly. I have many of these pets. I will have another soon. I've picked her out." Talib winked at him. "I must be patient, however; she has usefulness to one of my business partners. When she's no longer useful, I'll teach her lessons she'll never forget."

"You're attracted to a businesswoman? Really? I prefer mine a bit less schooled and less refined." The sounds of the whip against the woman's flesh continued. Thankfully, the man who was shoving his cock down the woman's throat had climaxed. Reaper swallowed hard to keep from growling.

Talib downed his second drink, and the handler came back in, leading three more women. "She's not a businesswoman. She is an artist. A crude, disgusting gutter wench who will learn to beg and then learn that begging doesn't work," Talib laughed drunkenly. "You and I should go out for dinner and talk about our interests."

"Is there a place where we won't be overheard?"

"Of course. Discretion is bought and paid for in Cannes. What hotel are you at? I'll call after I finish here."

Reaper gave him the information, but he wasn't sure if the bastard heard him. His eyes were pinned on the new women. "The redhead is good; she takes a lot of pain. The blonde bruises easily; you'll have to pay extra if you put too many on her. The dark-haired one is the one I'm taking today. She's always been busy when I've been here before. From what I heard, she can take every hole being stuffed and her nose pinched shut. She loves it. I want to break her. Wish me luck." Talib made his way to them and pointed at the dark-haired woman. He snapped on her leash, not to her neck but to the chain that ran between her breasts. Blindfolded, the woman stumbled as he pulled her violently toward the door.

The handler put the two other blindfolded women in corners and retrieved the woman who had been used and choked by the asshole in the chair. He led her out and shut the door. Reaper finished his bottle of water and sat the thing on the bar. Hoping his face looked utterly bored and unaffected, he strolled out of the library and headed back to the front of the building.

"Going so soon?" The woman who'd interviewed him earlier stepped out of a door.

"Indeed. Today, I was looking to see if my needs could be fulfilled here. It was enlightening. I will be back." And he'd bring the fucking French Foreign Legion with him to pull every abused woman out of this place, shut it down, and identify every abusive fuckwad that had ever graced the halls of this establishment. He didn't go off the books, but he knew an assassin who did, and she would take delight in castrating these bastards before she killed them.

"I look forward to your return." The madam of the house smiled up at him.

"Not as much as I do." He lifted a brow and then walked out.

CHAPTER 11

Reaper waited as the conference call connected to all the players. He poured another cup of coffee and wished like hell he was out of Cannes and in Paris. He had no doubt that someone from Guardian was watching Harmony, but unless he knew the operative, he'd question their techniques. Hell, even if he knew who was watching her, unless he was there and able to respond on a moment's notice, he wouldn't be happy. He took a sip of his coffee and shrugged. That was a lie. As long as she was involved in this mess, he wouldn't be happy.

"Archangel online." The familiar growly voice broke the silence.

"All parties online, sir. Operator Two-Seven-Four is clear."

"CCS, give us a rundown on what you've found."

"The video at the auction was enlightening, although it wasn't run like a typical auction. We do believe there were purchases made, just not the art," the woman spoke rapidly.

"Explain that," Archangel fired off.

"Well, money in the amounts indicated by the auctioneer was routed to shell company number thirty-five. We are in the process of reverse engineering where it came from, but that's as easy as finding a needle in a haystack. Unless I have unlimited access to over a thousand banks, transfer wires, and internet companies, it is almost impossible. Believe me, it is a lot easier to follow the money than retrace it."

"You said almost impossible," Fury pointed out.

"I did. I'm good. Screw it, I'm better than good, but it is going to take time and manpower. I'm assigning everyone I have that isn't currently active on other cases, so some of HR's low-priority hiring background requests are going to have to wait. I'd appreciate *someone* informing them of that fact."

He heard Archangel chuckle. "I'm on it. Make this happen for us."

"I'm working it. In the meantime, I've been able to identify a handful of the players from the video we received of the auction. Kudos to whoever was wearing the glasses. They got us just about every face, and they were the reason we were able to identify the dollar amounts spoken by the auctioneer and routed to the offshore account."

"There's no audio on the video." Reaper frowned as he stated the obvious.

"Lip reading." Bengal's wife filled in the gap in his understanding. "I've sent the names to the section heads via interoffice memo. The reason any of these people would be at an art auction is questionable. We have three generals of rogue nations, one right-hand man of a country on the brink of civil war, and another who we have very loosely linked to the IOU."

Reaper sagged back in his chair. The new kid on the block was the IOU, a terrorist group rumored to be gathering weapons and recruiting for a massive attack. Every intelligence agency in the world was trying to figure out what the group was up to and who it was targeting, but as of yet, it was just a rumor like Stratus and the Fates, only no one questioned the possibility that the IOU actually existed.

Finding someone linked to the organization was a huge step.

"Operative Fourteen, what did you find out from your primary?" Archangel filled the silence.

"Two things. First, this guy is one sick fu... ah, jerk who I'll gladly eliminate for free. Just say the word. Second, he said, and I'm quoting here, 'Even if you were as rich as David Xavier, you couldn't have won that auction. It wasn't intended for you.'"

"What does that mean?" the woman from CCS mused.

"I'm not sure, other than perhaps the auction was a front." Reaper sighed. "It's the only thing that makes sense. The paintings didn't go to the highest bidder. Several of the smaller paintings were sold repeatedly."

Fury gave a sharp laugh. "They weren't buying the paintings."

Archangel interrupted, "Unfortunately, until we know for a fact what they were buying, we can't move forward. Speculation and gut feelings work in the field, not when it comes to the Council."

Reaper nodded to himself. It was one of the many things that gave him faith in the process. The Council didn't act on suspicion. They operated on cold, hard facts, just like Guardian. That was his touchstone when it came to his work. It always would be.

"Like I don't know that." He could picture Fury rolling his eyes. Fury continued, "We have two assets in-country with Thirteen and Fourteen. Both are in Paris. One is covering the building where Ms. Flinn is residing during the day. The other has the night shift. She's important to one of ours, so she's being treated as family."

"Copy. Thirteen, update on your primary."

"He's a prima donna. He has guards with him at all times. I mean at *all* times. I went all princess on his ass, demanding they leave the room when we were getting... personal. He refused. I left. He's still on the hook. He's called me four different times today. I'll call him back after I get instructions."

"The residence is equipped with a labyrinth of hallways behind the rooms. I have the blueprints." Reaper offered the information.

"Kinky," Val chuckled. "I won't be able to work him for information; like I said, there are guards within earshot at all times, but if I can get the information from Reaper, I'll be able to take him as a target."

"Noted." Anubis spoke for the first time. "As of yet, we are still on hold. We need more information."

"We have another way." Reaper hated what he'd just said, but it was the truth. "Harmony. She has contact with LaVette. She can work him for information."

"She's a civilian. I don't want her compromised any further than she is." Archangel disregarded his suggestion.

"I know her, sir. She's tough. I think she can do this. As soon as Talib goes back to Paris, I'll be there. We can talk through comms and work together. She may know more than she thinks she does. I haven't had a chance to do a proper interview."

"What did we learn about the investigation and surveillance at the apartment where Ms. Flinn resides?"

Anubis chuckled. "There is only one door that opens to the apartment building: the front door. The back door has been painted shut. A sharp box cutter and you're in the building without being watched. Second, they don't have cameras or listening devices installed in the apartment, and we don't believe they have anyone in the apartments on her floor watching her. They do have a pressure plate installed under the three tiles directly in front of her door. Our asset was able to identify the apparatus because while the grout in all the building tile is flaking and missing, these three tiles were clear of all grout lines. It took a few seconds after that to find the pressure plate. We are assuming it alarms to an app on the phone for the person observing from outside or perhaps Behar or LaVette."

"So, we take out the observer and get her out." Val said the words he was thinking.

"If we do that, it will eliminate our ability to connect the dots," Archangel mused.

Reaper had one foot in each camp. He knew that Harmony could be out of that apartment and gone in a heartbeat. Every protective fiber in his body screamed for him to argue for that tactic. A softer voice replied to the rage, *And if you ask her to stay the information may save countless lives. She has an asset watching her.*

"Sir, I know her. When I get to Paris, let me speak to her. She's a strong woman. I think she'll stay the course as long as she knows we've got her back. If Talib becomes a direct threat to her, the asset watching her can intervene."

There was silence for a moment before Archangel spoke. "I'll table the decision until you're able to contact her and ascertain her willingness to help. CCS, work that backward cash flow. Fury, you didn't mention the medical team."

"They are en route and should land in Paris by nine tonight, Paris time. I can fly them down to Cannes or leave them in Paris. Your call."

"Any intel on the two primaries' travel plans?"

"My primary is staying here for the next three weeks. He invited me to Paris with him before I made him grovel. I'm sure the invitation will still be on once I let him crawl back."

Val's update made him chuckle. The woman used everything she had when she was working a case. Her beauty was a tool to her, nothing more. She wasn't a vain person. Her looks were just an asset she could utilize.

"Talib is scheduled to return to Paris the day after tomorrow on the red-eye flight out of Cannes. He made the reservation about thirty minutes ago," Bengal's woman interjected.

"Reaper, do you have Talib's contact information?"

"I do."

"Use it. I want the information that man knows. We have several chemical options."

"He's a sloppy drunk. I'll need a vial of something that works with bourbon. I'll need him to remain upright but be open to questioning." Reaper would take him out for a drink, slip the chemical into his drink, and then interrogate him.

"I'll have it to you tomorrow by noon," Anubis informed him quickly.

"I want an update on that conversation as soon as humanly possible. We are still in the information-gathering phase of this op. All codes are on hold."

"Copy that," Reaper answered.

"Understood," Val echoed his response.

"Archangel out."

"CCS Out."

"The Rose is out."

"Do you have any questions?" Anubis asked.

"Who is on the building?"

"Fifteen and Seventeen." His handler's response was immediate.

Phoenix, Fifteen, and Harbinger, Seventeen. Reaper drew a deep, refreshing breath. He could rest easier now. Those two men would move heaven and earth for him as he would for them. "Thank you."

"No worries. Thirteen, I'm going on record with this. Sexual activity with this man is not required. Walk away."

"You say that like having sex with this man would be a hardship." She gave that low throaty laugh.

"As long as you understand this is not a requirement from us."

"I do. I have no doubt as to what is required and what isn't. I am comfortable with my position in this matter."

"Understood. Fourteen, do you need anything other than the chemicals?"

"Unfettered access on the comms to Harmony."

"I'll let the operator know you can patch through unmonitored at any time. Call me as soon as you get the information from Talib."

"Roger."

"We'll keep her safe in Paris, you two stay out of hot water. Whatever it takes."

"As long as it takes," he spoke at the same time as Val.

"The Annex is clear."

He cleared the call and smiled when his phone vibrated immediately. "I've talked to you more on this mission than I have in the last year."

"Whatever. If you don't get her out of this mess, you'll regret it. What if something happens to her?"

He sighed and stared at his shoes. "Val, what happens if we get her out and we don't find out what the auctions are about? You kill Ardan. What if he is just a small cog in a grand scheme?"

"Oh, believe me, his cog is very small."

She purred the response and he spit out a laugh. "I'll give Harmony the straight scoop. Well, as straight as I can without revealing too much. My hunch is she'll want to stay to see those two become smudges on the Paris streets."

"Oh, being hit by a truck. I haven't arranged one of those before. Let me do it? Please?"

"You worry about Ardan. I'll dead drop that map. The first beach chair next to the towel cabana at your hotel. Two this afternoon."

"Perfect. Now, I must call my primary before he becomes so distraught at my non-attention that he kills himself and I lose my shot at fun. Ciao, my friend."

He wasn't given a chance to answer. He dropped his phone to the table and stared out the window of his hotel's suite. He'd present the facts to Harmony. If she wanted out, he'd help her get out. If she'd stay and help them, he'd make sure she was safe. Either way, she'd be safe. He closed his eyes and drew a deep breath in. He'd handle business here and then make his way to Paris, to Harmony, and, hopefully, to the end of that slimy bastard, Talib.

CHAPTER 12

Harmony stood beside the one-slice toaster and waited for her baguette. Her shoulders ached and her eyes burned, but she'd made good progress on the painting. Although it was difficult work, the flow she could get into when working sometimes overrode other things such as food and water. She chugged the last half of the plastic cup she'd filled moments ago and refilled it again.

She wandered into the small living room and stared out the window, taking smaller sips of her water now that her immediate thirst had been quenched. The sun was setting and the white plaster of the building across the street took on a golden hue. It was a transformative time in Paris. The bustle of the day mellowed as the lushness of the evening grew. The city of lights, of romance, and of love. She sighed and shook her head. She'd never be able to picture the city that way. To her, Paris would always be tied to Talib, and Bernard, and her own ridiculous desire to be anywhere but Lake Garden.

She'd kicked herself a thousand times for taking the chance, for using the money from selling her aunt and uncle's farm to pay for this abysmal little apartment. But there were no other options. Certainly not in Lake Garden. She'd been labeled a pariah by the Grahams. They knew Roman had killed Bert, but they couldn't prove it. She'd learned to avoid town after she'd graduated. Leaving the farm meant she was subjected to the stares and not-so-subtle whispers of the townspeople. She'd thought the vitriol would die down, but the Grahams were fantastic at holding a grudge against her because she was Roman's girlfriend. Hell, they put a sharp edge on the damn thing and used it to cut her out of her own community. But that was her cross to bear. Roman *had* killed Bert. She'd seen the aftermath with her own eyes. The man had no right to taunt Roman. Roman said the man admitted to murdering both his father and Tom. She sighed and went back to the tiny kitchen. She drank her water and then filled the plastic tumbler with some of the wine she'd opened yesterday after work. She took her food and wine back to her couch and tucked into it.

Maggie was the only one who'd never paid attention to the Grahams. That's why they'd brought in the community center and had free healthcare. Not that Maggie seemed to care, but she was the only friend Harmony still had in the small town. Her cousin Delbert was convinced that Roman had killed Bert. She never said a word to anyone about Roman. Well, with the exception of Maggie. She told Maggie how much she missed him. She knew how to keep her mouth shut. No one would ever prosecute Roman unless he confessed, which time had proven he wasn't going to do.

Brushing the toast crumbs off her shirt onto her small plastic plate, she relaxed on the couch and watched the sun paint deeper and darker colors on the white plaster across the way. She thought of the Roman she knew. The hot-tempered boy who fought for her, fought bullies, and fought injustices at school. His heart was pure. His temper was what got him into trouble. She used to know everything about him. She could tell when he was upset without him having to say a word. The way his eyes tightened around the corners and his lips tugged down spoke volumes to her. If he cocked his head to the right, whoever he was talking to was going to get punched. The twitch at the corner of his mouth when he was teasing her and the way his eyes lit up when she fell for whatever bull he was shoveling her way were imprinted in her mind and on her heart. He was the boy of her dreams until a nightmare tore them apart.

When the apartment was totally dark, she pulled herself from her memories. Standing up to take her dish to the sink, she padded into the kitchen.

"Harmony?"

She screamed, throwing her plate into the air and spinning around. Nobody was there. She touched her ear and gasped, "Holy shit! Damn it! Stop freaking doing that! I'm going to die of a heart attack!"

Roman's low chuckle rolled through the earpiece.

"It's not funny!"

"It kind of is." His laughing response pulled at her, too.

"Seriously, can you make a clicky sound or a beep or something? I was taking my plate to the sink in the dark and boom, all of a sudden, I hear my name right here. I'm telling you, I may not live until long enough to get out of this mess. Between you and the operator, I'm going to stroke out." She bent down and picked up her plastic plate, tossing it into the tiny sink.

"What operator?"

"I don't know, she didn't tell me her name, just that they'd be listening all the time. Hey, operator, are you listening now?"

"I am indeed." The operator's response held a tinge of laughter.

"She thinks it's funny, too," Roman chuckled. "Thank you, but I've got it for now. I'll let you know when you need to resume monitoring."

"Affirmative, Fourteen, I have your authorization listed. Enjoy. Operator Two-Seven-Four is clear."

Harmony turned on a small table lamp in her living room and sat down on the couch. "You said you'd have answers for me when you called back."

"I have a few. Not as many as we'd like."

"What does that mean?" She closed her eyes and dropped her head back onto the couch.

Roman pulled a deep breath of air before he responded. "We don't know much more than we knew when we talked before. Stringing what happened at the auction to events around the world is taking time."

She opened her eyes and stared at the roof. There

was a water stain in the corner that had been growing since she arrived. One day, that corner of the roof would fall in. Hopefully, she'd be gone before that happened. "Do me a favor, yeah? Just put it out there. I'm so tired of trying to figure out what is going on, to read between the lines, you know? I just need you to level with me."

"All right. We'd like you to stay in the apartment and continue to work for LaVette. When LaVette or Behar come over, we'd like you to get information from them about what's happening at the auction or about who will be there."

"Right. I'll invite them over tomorrow, and we'll have coffee and talk about the ins and outs of their blackmail operation. That's not how this works, Roman. I do what they tell me when they tell me to do it." She rubbed her neck. The bruises were yellow and green now, but they were still there every time she looked in the mirror.

"I understand that. I'm not asking you to perform an interrogation, just talk to them."

"Talib better not come here, or there won't be much talking going on. I'll be too busy trying to kill him." She pulled her legs up under her. She had weapons in the apartment. Several knives in the kitchen. Pallet knives in the studio. A heavy glass vase in the bedroom alcove along with her keys that she kept by the bed. She'd planned out how to get to each of them if she needed to defend herself. If she couldn't get to the weapons, she knew where to hit a guy so it would hurt the worst. Balls, eyes, nose, and ears. She wasn't big, but she was strong from years working the farm. What she lacked in stature, she'd make up in ingenuity. "Besides, Bernard and I struck an agreement. I work my ass off and he keeps Talib away from me."

"Do you believe he'll keep his end of the agreement?"

She blinked at the question. Did she? *Well, I had until just this second.* "I guess he doesn't have a good track record." And damn it, that was a problem, wasn't it? "I'll stay and see it through. I want both Bernard and Talib behind bars. What they are doing is unconscionable. If I can stop this from happening to another person, it'll be worth the next thirty days or so in hell." She tucked back into the cushions of the couch, feeling the weight of the commitment she'd just made.

"We have people watching you. People I trust. We'll make sure that nothing happens. If Talib makes a move in your apartment's direction, we'll know about it. Besides, he isn't even in Paris right now. I will let you know when he gets back into town." Roman's growl carried a possessiveness she hadn't heard in a long time.

"So, tell me what has happened to you in the last ten years." She wanted to know every detail. She'd imagined him working in the city. She'd even daydreamed that he'd come down her driveway in a big truck, open the door, and declare his love for her. Then he'd sweep her off her feet, bundle her into the vehicle, and drive them far away from Lake Garden.

"There isn't a lot I *can* tell. I've signed documentation keeping the majority of what I do between my employer and myself. What I can tell you is that I've realized the dream I had when I was a boy. I wanted to make a difference. I wanted to be the person who stood up for those who couldn't stand up for themselves." He gave a small burst of laughter.

"You got into a lot of fights protecting kids from bullies." Roman was the protector of all the misfits. He didn't let the popular kids, the kids with money, pick on those who didn't have any.

"And I won all of them." There was pride that she could plainly hear in his voice.

"Yes, but you usually ended up at Maggie's." She

chuckled, remembering all of the stitches, butterfly bandages, and cut lips that Maggie had taken care of.

"That's only because Tom would drop at the sight of blood." Roman's laughter filled her ear.

"True. A strange combination for a farmer." She chuckled as well. "He had a heart as big as the sky, though."

"I miss him. I was with him longer than I was with my dad. They both hold an equal place in my life." The softness of his voice was so reminiscent of the boy she once knew.

"So, you take care of the underdog. Is it rewarding? Is it everything you thought it would be?" She prayed it was.

"There are advantages and disadvantages. Is it rewarding? Yes. Is it everything I thought it would be? Let's just say it's different than I thought it would be. Those high school dreams of wearing a badge and carrying a gun, where I drove around in a patrol car and didn't get my hands dirty, that was a pipe dream. Ensuring people who cannot take care of themselves are protected is complicated, dirty, exhausting work. The training that I was put through is the best in the world. It is also the hardest. For three years, I did nothing but train and sleep. There was no chance to come back. After that, I was dropped knees-deep into a world I thought I understood. Boy, was I wrong. I'm sorry I didn't come back for you, Harmony. It was and is my greatest regret."

"Well, there is still that unresolved issue. The one that drove you away. I knew you could never come back, but I did dream of the time that you would sneak back to town and whisk me away." A tear dropped over her lower lid. "I missed you so damn much. In one day, I lost my best friend and my lover." Her heart broke that day. While she had healed, the pieces of her heart still lay in total disarray. Not that she couldn't have moved on; she could have. The men who had asked her out were gentlemen. They treated her well, but none of them were Roman.

"You probably were put through hell when I left. I can't imagine the Grahams being kind to anyone who was associated with me. The last time I spoke to Maggie, she told me they still blame me for Bert's death."

She wiped the tear before it could drip from her chin. "Oh, you could say that." He could say a hell of a lot more. It had taken five years before she felt at ease when she left the farm and went to the grocery store. Every time she'd gone into town, someone would say something. But the passing of time seemed to dull the fun of tormenting her. Thank God.

"I'd hoped that you would have found someone." He groaned and admitted, "That's bullshit. As much as I wanted you to be happy, I would've died inside if you had found somebody."

"What about you? Did you find someone?" She drew a ragged breath and held it.

"No. There's only been you. There'll only ever be you. You're the light that shines on my darkness. You're my hope when I can't find a way forward. You always have been. We've shared the best times and the hardest moments of our lives. No one, Harmony, *no one* has ever taken your place in my heart."

She released the breath in her lungs as more tears tripped over the bottom lashes of her eyes. "I love you, Roman."

"I never stopped loving you. Soon, we'll be done with Bernard and Talib. I'll take some time off, and we will find a way forward for us. Somehow, the universe has thrown us together half the world away from Lake Garden. I'm never going to let you go again." His voice held a raspy edge of emotion.

"I wish you were here right now. I really need to

feel your arms around me." She snuffled a bit and wiped at her tears.

"I know. Believe me, babe, I need to hold you as desperately as you need to be held. Unfortunately, we're going to have to wait. Just a bit longer." Roman's voice held the same anguish hers held. "We managed ten years; we can handle another thirty days."

She laughed with him. "Will you call or whatever this is again tomorrow?"

"Not tomorrow. I'll be working. But if you need anything, just ask the operator. She is always listening."

"How is that possible? She said she was human, but how is she *always* listening?"

Roman's laughter pulled a smile to her lips. "That has been a point of speculation within our company for as long as anyone can remember. Her voice never changes, she always knows who's calling, and is usually two steps ahead of everyone. It's freaky."

"Well, I'm glad I'm not the only one who questioned the premise." She ran her thumbnail down the corded line of the fabric in the couch. "This is real, right? I'm not dreaming this, am I? And don't laugh at me, but when good things happen to me lately, it turns to shit really fast."

"You're not dreaming, but as late as it is, you should be. I'm not going to lie, this mess could turn ugly fast, but we have people watching, and they will be there if you need them."

"You're sure?" She glanced out the window, barely able to see the building across the street.

"I am. I need to disconnect the comms now. The operator will resume monitoring. I love you, Harmony."

"I love you, too. Call me, or earpiece me, when you can." She didn't mean to sound as needy as she did, but damn it, he was in her life again. Who could blame her?

"And make clicking sounds before I say your name, right?"

"Oh, my God! You cannot tease me about that. My heart literally skipped a beat! I swear that is the freakiest thing. How do you get used to it?" She pushed up to the edge of the couch and lifted her hand in the darkness, gesturing wildly.

Roman's rumble of laughter filled her ear. "When you live with it you get used to it. Good night, Harmony. You're safe, and I love you."

"I love you, too." She stood and glanced at the small bed in the alcove. Roman was right, she should get some rest. But now that the creative muse inside her had been illuminated, there was something she wanted to paint. No, *needed* to paint.

She made her way back into her studio, turned on the light, and pulled a fresh canvas from the back of the stack. Her mind's eye was already painting Roman's features. His strong chin, straight nose, and high, defined cheekbones were in the perfect position. His eyes... His eyes were filled with love. She knew that expression. The man had matured, but she knew how to paint the love she felt at this moment. Roman was her definition of love. He always had been.

CHAPTER 13

R eaper entered the upscale bar in the resort's main lobby. Talib had invited him over for a drink. His upper lip lifted into a snarl for a split second. He'd met some disgusting people in the last ten years and had helped the world by eliminating many of them, but Talib took the prize for the most worthless, non-targetable scum that he'd ever had the displeasure of meeting. The sleaze factor oozed off the man like snake oil off a charlatan.

The man lifted his hand from a booth at the back of the establishment. Reaper headed his way and unbuttoned his suit jacket before he sat down across from the piece of human garbage. In French, he greeted his acquaintance, "I'm surprised you wanted to meet here, I would have assumed the distractions at 1859 would have been more to our mutual liking."

Talib motioned for the waiter. "Much. Unfortunately, the management at the establishment have requested I not return." He waved his hand in the air dismissively. "It will be fixed soon."

The waiter arrived just as Talib finished his comment. Reaper looked at the man. "Scotch, single malt, neat, and make it decent, please, none of that American crap."

Talib laughed like a loon. "But you're American."

"I'm an American with taste." Reaper batted back the banter to Talib. "Why were you asked not to come back?"

"Bah, an infraction of the rules of the house. I supposedly left injuries that will scar." He leaned forward. "But there are those of us who prefer to see the scars. They show obedience can be learned."

Reaper smiled and cocked his head, giving an almost imperceptible dip of his chin in agreement. Behind his calm nod, he craved the physical destruction of the bastard across from him. His drink arrived, and he swirled it in the crystal glass. "What do you intend to do with the rest of your time in Cannes? Go to the beach?" Reaper took a sip of the scotch.

"Unfortunately, no. I'm leaving for Paris. Tonight will be my last night to kick up my heels, as it were."

"A shame you can't go back to 1859."

Talib leaned forward. "I will. Money fixes everything. It will assuage the proprietor's ruffled feathers. With enough money, one can get away with murder."

Reaper lifted an eyebrow and smiled. "Hypothetically speaking, of course."

Talib snorted. "Of course." He lifted his hand for the waiter, caught the man's eye, and circled his finger, indicating another round for each of them.

"How long will you be in Paris? I have business there at the end of the month."

"I live there. A must for the drudgery my work requires me to do."

"Ah, that's right. Auctions." Reaper drawled the last word, belittling it.

"Not just auctions. It is more than you think." Talib accepted his next drink and caught the waiter before he left. "Another round."

"In a hurry to get drunk?" Reaper leaned back with his original scotch.

"In a hurry to be done with Cannes. When you come to Paris, I will show you the places that cater to men like us. I don't often invite others to play with me, but as we have similar tastes, perhaps I'll make an exception."

"I prefer to work alone, but perhaps. It sounds… intriguing." *Sickening. Sadistic. Disturbed.* The adjectives could go on forever.

Talib turned in his seat. "Where is that waiter?" He waved at the man again. The waiter acknowledged him but didn't come over. "This is preposterous. I'll be back." Talib slid out of the booth and headed toward the bar.

Reaper reached into his pocket, flipped the top on the vial, and slipped the chemicals into Talib's crystal tumbler. He'd just pocketed the vial when Talib returned with two more drinks. The man downed the two in his hands quickly. Their conversation centered around Paris and Talib's favorite haunts.

"To leaving Cannes and its bothersome rules." He tipped back the tumbler.

Reaper took a sip of his first scotch. "To leaving Cannes."

Talib placed the tumbler on the table. He blinked at the glass and then lifted his head, looking at Reaper. "I don't feel well."

Reaper sighed. "Give me your key card, I'll help you up to your room."

Talib nodded stupidly, handing over his card. "1204." The numbers slurred together.

Reaper stood and pocketed the room card. He grabbed Talib's arm and pulled him out of the bench. The waiter appeared as he grabbed the man to keep him from falling. "Please, charge the drinks to his room. 1204. Give yourself a generous tip."

The waiter smiled and nodded. "Thank you, sir. Do you need assistance?"

Reaper shook his head. "It is his standard pattern. I'll just dump him in his room so he can sober up."

The waiter moved and Reaper half-carried, half-dragged the semi-conscious man to the elevator. The trip up to the 12th floor was punctuated by Talib's drunken laughter. "Stupid people. You don't know. I'm invincible."

"Sure, you are." Reaper dragged the man down the hall and dumped Talib against the wall, pinning him there with the side of his body as he opened the door. He pulled the man into his suite and plopped him into a chair. He reached into his pocket and took out the second vial, poured it into a tumbler, and handed it to Talib. "Drink this."

The man didn't even hesitate; he upended the tumbler, drinking it all. Reaper took the tumbler and rinsed it out at the bar sink and made his way back to Talib. "What is your name?"

"Talib Pierre Malecon Behar."

"What do you do for your father in Paris?"

That maniacal laughter again. "Not much."

"What do the paintings that are bid on represent?"

"Who cares?"

"Who knows what they represent?"

"I don't know."

"Do Ardan and your father work together?"

"Maybe. I don't know what my father did."

Reaper tried another tactic. "Are the auctions where Ardan and your father work together?"

Talib nodded and then shook his head.

"Why do you need the masters copied?"

"Payment."

Reaper squinted at the drugged man. *What did he mean?* "Explain that."

"The paintings are payment."

"To whom?"

Talib shook his head. "Must be perfect. The stage must be perfect for the performers."

"Who are the performers?"

Talib's head rolled back on his shoulders. "Me. The world is a stage."

"Who bids on the paintings?"

"I don't know. People with enough money."

Reaper sat there and stared at the incapacitated degenerate while he put the information Talib had given him together. The man had provided nothing new. So, they were back to the basics. The key was what the paintings being bid on represented. If Talib didn't know, it served to follow that Bernard didn't either.

"Why did you take your painter to Cannes?"

"Ardan. He wanted to see her. After she's done, he'd buy her."

"Buy her?"

Talib snorted. "He trades women for favors. She's pretty."

"I thought you wanted to break her."

"Ardan doesn't care. She'll be experienced at what is required of her when I'm done."

"Have you ever killed a woman?"

"Many." Talib's head dropped down and bounced back up, his eyes barely open.

"Your father covered the murders with money and made them go away."

Talib's head bounced up and down. He glanced at his watch. The chemicals would knock the man out soon, and he'd wake with a bitch of a headache but no recollection of anything after he drank the first vial.

He hauled the man to his feet, took off his jacket, flung it on a chair, and dropped the key card on top of it. He pushed Talib to the bedroom and dropped him onto the bed. With caution and care, he wiped down everything he'd touched in the room, including the keycard. Was it necessary? No. Was it in his nature? Absolutely. He opened the suite door, protecting his hand with a paper napkin he'd taken off the bar. When the door shut behind him, he crumpled up the napkin and placed it in his pocket as he headed to the elevator. He had a report to make.

Jacob King glanced at the information on the screen. "Ardan's weapons."

His wife, Tori, nodded. "I received the information from the CIA. These serial numbers were in the lot stolen from the freighter pirates seized off the coast of Africa. Ardan's crew was rumored to be the mastermind behind that operation. The CIA and ICE have confirmed with corroborating evidence."

"Where were they found?"

"In Tsleznia."

Jacob turned to look at his wife. "The country that stopped a coup attempt yesterday."

Jewell's voice from the speaker chimed in. "The same. We have a kind of connection to the Cannes operation. Monitor six."

Tori hissed when the picture flashed up. "Damn it, Jewell."

"Oh, shit. Sorry. I've been looking at him all day. I forgot to warn you," Jewell apologized.

Jacob put his hand on his wife's shoulder as he stared at the picture. A man with literally half his face missing was larger than life on monitor six. "How is this unfortunate soul related to the Cannes operation?"

"Well, facial recognition is confused on this guy. You know it works off of key factors like the depth of eye sockets and the distance between your eyes, distance between your chin and your forehead, right? He has half a face. That distance can't be confirmed, but it did hit on two points. If the program is right, he was on the Pissarro's bidder's right at the auction."

"Two out of eight points isn't a verified identification." Tori shook her head. "I'd hesitate to stamp confirmation on the computer's results."

"Yeah, that's what I thought, too. But I forwarded it to the Annex and to Jason. Another data point for them to consider."

"What about the mercenaries that were killed?" Jacob asked his sister.

"We have three or four confirmed identities. Tori, I'm sending you the names. Jason wants to see if the CIA has anything on these guys. There is nothing in our databases, but we don't track terrorists for a living. Well, not these little guys, anyway."

He heard Jewell's fingers flying across her keyboard.

Tori switched screens and pulled up the interoffice communication. "I've got it. Give me a minute, I have access to that CIA database."

"Cool. How'd you manage that?" Jewell chirped the question.

"They got tired of me sending requests over."

Jacob chuckled, and Tori looked up and winked at him. He remembered that month. Tori had made it her mission to gain access to the database and sent over request after request. Finally, Cole Davis, the deputy director of overseas operations and their liaison to Guardian, called Jason and told him he'd allow access but only to Tori, who would process all of Guardian's searches.

"Here, they have two listed. I'll package this and send it to the Annex. They can distribute to whoever has the need to know."

Jewell spoke, "Send it to me, too. The more information I have, the better I work."

"I already did." Tori chuckled her response.

"You know me so well. I got to go, so much to do and not enough time to do it. Toodles."

Jacob didn't even bother saying goodbye. His sister had already disconnected. "In all of this mess," he indicated the computer screens and the printouts on Tori's desk, "we need to find a tie-in to the senior Behar. Ardan has been given a stay of execution. We don't want to drive Behar into hiding by taking Ardan out, but the Council isn't going to wait forever. Somewhere in here is the key. It has to be."

"Then let's start with the anomalies. What doesn't make sense? What is the biggest red flag here?" Tory cleared away the paperwork and pulled her keyboard toward her.

"Behar and Ardan working together." Jacob spoke and Tori typed. "They don't have any connection that we are aware of."

"Has Jewell worked this angle?" Tori entered her password to the CCS system.

"No, not that I know."

"Okay, we'll start there. We'll scour their backgrounds and try to find similarities and look for a connection. If we can connect them socially or through business, we have a thread." Her fingers flew over the keyboard.

"Have I told you how much I miss you being here full-time?"

Tori glanced up and smiled at him. "I miss it too, but not as much as I'd miss being home with the kids after school and on weekends."

"You juggle a hell of a lot." Jacob sat down and pulled out another keyboard for the secondary system on her workstation.

"We all do. Oh, Talon's baseball coach called yesterday. He wants to nominate him for the traveling team."

Jacob stopped typing. "That would take you out of the local area."

"Yep, but he's good, Jacob. His pitching is phenomenal."

"Not exaggerating there are you?"

"Not even a tiny bit." Tori laughed and nudged his shoulder with hers. "Let's look at the schedule and see if it's doable. The coach hasn't told Talon, so he won't be disappointed if we can't make it work."

"Sounds like a plan. Between all of us, though, we

should be able to have someone with him." Hell, Talon had more than enough aunts and uncles in D.C. He wasn't above calling in some favors to make sure his kid got the honor of being on a traveling team. Playing the best of the best would only help his game.

"There, now we'll let Godzilla chomp on the data and see what it spits out." Tori pushed the keyboard back.

Jacob turned and dropped a kiss on Tori's lips. "Have I told you today how much I love you?"

She smiled. "Once or twice. Now, get to work, mister. I don't want to be late getting home."

CHAPTER 14

Harmony laughed at the clicks that sounded in her ear. "Is that you snapping your fingers?" She poured a glass of wine as she spoke.

"It was indeed. What are you doing tonight?"

"Well, I had a great day on the painting, got more done than I had anticipated, so I am celebrating with a glass of wine. One of the perks of being in France. Check that. The only perk of living in France. Many bottles of wine delivered twice a week with my groceries." At least, it was the only benefit for her. She turned and leaned against the kitchen counter. "What are you doing?"

"I'm working. Also, Talib landed in Paris about two hours ago."

"Awesome." She glanced at the door. The chain

was still connected. She *knew* the man had a key to her apartment.

"We'll have someone watching."

Roman's assurance was great, but… "So, changing the subject. Tell me how you got hooked up with this security company."

"Long story. The recruiter found me and took me under his wing. He thought I'd be a good fit for the company, and since the training gave me a place to live, food, and paid me, I sure as hell wasn't going to… ah, there we go. I wasn't going to turn it down."

"What are you doing? Are you at work right *now*?"

"I am working and right now I'm eliminating a barrier. Why?"

"I have no idea what that means."

Roman chuckled. "You will. Have you talked to Maggie lately?"

"No, I know she'll read me like an open book if I call. She'll hop on a plane and come over if she thinks I'm in trouble."

"Knowing that old woman, she'd do it if she doesn't hear from you, too." Roman's voice echoed a bit.

"Probably. Are you in a tin can? You're echoing."

"No, I'm in a wicked small stairwell."

"Ha, you don't know wicked small until you've seen the stairway in my building. There has to be like a billion building code infractions in this place." She glanced up at the growing wet spot on the ceiling of her apartment. It amazed her how much grip that plaster had.

"Probably two billion," Roman agreed.

"Hey, you haven't seen it. Don't be so judgmental, that's my job." She laughed and took a sip of her wine.

"Harmony, will you do me a favor?"

"I don't know. The last favor you asked me to do is keeping me in this hell hole for twenty-eight more days."

"Trust me, I think you'll like this favor."

"Uh-huh. Okay, hit me with it."

"Open your front door."

"What?"

"Open your front door."

She put down the wine and walked over to the door. "Did you send me something?"

"I did."

She slid the chain back and undid the deadbolt, opening the door a tiny bit. She looked down at the tile in front of her door, expecting to see a box.

Instead, Roman was standing in the hall.

"Roman!" She squealed his name.

He held out a hand, and she froze. "Back up."

Her brow creased in concern, but she moved back. Roman stepped over the tile directly in front of her door and into her apartment.

"Why did you jump like that?" She whispered the words.

"A pressure plate under the tile at the front of your door." He shut the door and flipped the lock. "Come here." He held his arms open wide, and she flew to him.

His big body swallowed her up as he hugged her, but it was the best feeling in the world. She held him in a strangulation hold and laughed and cried at the same time. One of his hands stroked her hair, the other held her tight to him.

Finally able to believe he was holding her, she tilted her head up, wanting a kiss but not knowing how to ask for it. It had been ten years. She loved him, or at least who he was.

He lowered to her mouth, his eyes searching hers as he moved. Finally, his lips touched hers, and she melted into the sensation of their kiss. His tongue swiped her lips and she opened for him. The scent of him was familiar and ignited ten years of latent passion. The kiss went from searching to urgent in less than a second. She practically crawled up the man. He reached down and grabbed her ass, lifting her up. She wrapped her legs around him, securing her higher position. They kissed until she couldn't breathe.

Parting, she moved back enough to see him. "Take me to bed, Roman."

"Are you sure? That's not the reason I'm here…" She put a finger over his lips and stilled his words. He leaned forward and kissed her again but broke away before it got too hot.

"I've never been more sure about anything in my life."

He glanced around the tiny apartment, and she saw when he zeroed in on the twin bed.

He walked over to it with her still wrapped around him. She let her legs drop to the floor. Roman broke the kiss and dropped to his knees. He raised the t-shirt she wore and kissed the skin above the waistband of her jeans. Tiny prickles of goose-flesh lifted over her skin. He pulled on the shirt as he kissed her. She tugged it off and let it drop. Roman's tongue traced a line along the edge of her waistband. She dropped her hands to his shoulders. The muscles under her hands were stronger, his shoulders were broader, but the man making her crazy with need wasn't different.

This was Roman.

Her Roman.

She ran her fingers through his hair as he unfastened and unzipped her jeans. She moved so the denim could fall. He helped her step out of the material as he nipped, kissed, and licked the thin strip of elastic lace at the top of her panties. He pulled them down past her hips and let them fall to the floor. Roman slid his hands up her ribs and cupped her breasts, his thumbs rasping over her hardened nipples under the thin cotton of her bra. He stood and unhooked it. She let the thing drop off her arms and stood completely naked in front of her lover.

He lifted his shirt off and dropped it on the floor as she had. *My God. His muscles have muscles.* Toeing out of his boots as his hands unfastened his jeans, he stripped out of his clothes in seconds. She stared at the rippling muscle and the mat of dark brown hair on his chest. The thin trail continued lower and drew her attention down to his cock. Maturity hadn't changed him in this area. His shaft was heavy, thick, and long. She stepped forward and cupped him in one hand while the other fondled his balls, just the way he'd taught her to do.

The years of separation melted. She leaned forward and licked at one of the flat bronze disks on his chest while she stroked her hand up and down.

His hands threaded through her hair in a familiar possessive move before he tilted her head back and seized her lips. Delving into his kiss, losing herself in the ecstasy of the man she loved, she barely noticed as he lowered them onto the bed. He split her legs with one of his and she opened for him.

He lifted away suddenly. "Shit. Condom."

She pulled him back down. "I'm on the pill. Don't stop."

He dropped down for a kiss as he entered her. She arched under him; the fullness was intense in the best possible way. She wrapped her legs around his and held on as his hips pistoned and his body worked its magic inside hers. He shifted one leg forward, breaking her ankle hold at the back of his thighs. He lifted one of her legs to his hip and slid forward again. Her eyes rolled back, and an unbidden moan of pleasure escaped. Roman dropped to capture her lips as he stroked inside of her. He supported himself on one elbow and snaked his free hand between them, fingering her clit.

Red and white blotches formed and disappeared from behind her clenched eyelids as her body contracted. She broke the kiss and cranked a death grip on Roman's arms as she shattered. She gasped, turned, and bit his arm, stifling her sounds of pleasure as she panted through her orgasm. Just as she caught her breath, that magical hand reappeared and Roman took her lips again. She rocked under him, meeting his thrusts with her hips. His fingers found the spot to the side of her clit and rubbed. Her body, already primed from the first orgasm, reached the apex again just before Roman slammed home and growled through his body's own release.

Roman pulled out and moved them so he was on the bed, Harmony draped over his chest. His breathing returned to normal long before hers did. She shuddered with the aftershock of those wonderful orgasms.

"Sorry, I bit you."

He stroked her hair. "You bit me twice and I love it."

She sighed, "God, that was way better than I remembered."

His laugh rumbled under her ear. "I'm not sure if I'm being complimented or insulted."

"Oh, 'twas a compliment, sir." She patted his shoulder and marveled once again at the solid muscle under her hand. They laid together for several long moments. She smiled at the wonder and familiarity of their after-sex cuddle.

His hand stroked down the length of her hair.

"Roman?"

"Yes?"

"I know you can't tell me much, but what exactly do you do for this security company?"

His hand never stopped its up-and-down slide over her hair. She didn't rush his reply; even as a kid, Roman took his time to answer. He had to be sure of what he was going to say whereas she just blurted things out.

"I'm a specialist who eliminates problems for management."

"What kind of problems?" She lifted up and dropped her chin on her cupped fist.

He glanced up at her. "I can't say."

"Huh." She stared down at him for a moment before she tried another tactic. "Are Talib and Bernard the type of problems you'd eliminate?"

His eyebrows lifted and he turned to look at her. "No. They aren't." He stared at her.

"Oh, I recognize that look."

He pulled back and frowned. "What look?"

"The 'I'm not going to tell you so don't keep asking me' look." She smiled when he rolled his eyes.

"These problems. When you eliminate them, do they ever reappear?"

"Never. I provide permanent solutions to the problems my employers expect me to fix." Roman turned onto his side, dumping her next to him on the twin bed. He hugged her close and moved his leg between hers, keeping them both on the small bed. "Why are you so curious?"

She reached up and pushed his bangs off his face. His dark brown hair fell through her fingers in a silky drape. How could she explain it without coming off as needy? Whatever, now was not the time to start being coy with the person who was her best friend for most of her life. "Because I don't know anything about what you've done in the last ten years. You know exactly where I was and what I was doing. You're a mystery and that scares me. What if I'm not enough for you anymore?"

He reached between them and held her chin in his fingers. "I tried my damnedest to forget you. I tried everything I knew to stop myself from driving north every time I was back in the States to check up on you. I'd park in the woods and stare at the house until I saw you. Until I knew you were okay. Not enough? My God, you are in every cell of my body. My entire life is built around you and no amount of time or distance will ever change that. You are what makes me whole."

A tear fell as she stared at him. "Why did fate tear us apart? Every day, I looked down that damn gravel road and prayed you'd come get me. You're my best friend, my first lover, and time hasn't diminished the way I feel about you. You are my world, Roman. You're everything I need to be happy."

He pulled her to his chest. The sound of his words rumbled under her ear, "Perhaps we needed to grow individually out of each other's shadow to understand the depth of what we had."

"Have." She closed her eyes and sighed in contentment as he hummed quietly in agreement. For the first time since he left Lake Garden all those years ago, she *knew* everything was going to be all right.

CHAPTER 15

Reaper leaned down and kissed Harmony. She stirred, lifted up to her elbows, and blinked up at him. "You're leaving?"

He smiled and cupped her cheek in his palm. She was so fucking beautiful. That light spray of freckles that dusted her nose and those beautiful hazel-green eyes had been in his memories and dreams for the last ten years. "If Bernard were to come over, my presence would be difficult to explain."

She dropped back into bed. "Damn it."

"I'll come back."

"Tonight?" Her eyes popped wide open and she lifted back up. The sheet slid down her body, revealing her high, tight breasts.

He leaned forward and placed a kiss on the top

swell of her breast. "I'll try, but I can't promise. Work may interfere."

She slid her hand through his hair and lifted up for a kiss. "It's still dark. Stay for a little longer?"

He groaned and shook his head, lifting away from the temptress wrapped in nothing but a thin sheet. "I have to go." He dipped down quickly and kissed her soundly on the lips before he stood, turned, and headed to the apartment door. "Lock up after me." He stopped at the door and drank in the vision of Harmony. His Harmony. She sat up, holding the sheet to her chest. Her long blonde hair fell over her shoulders, and the first beams of the morning sun shone through the window, casting a light behind her. "You look like an angel."

She smiled at him. "I'm no angel. I'm still the same woman, a bit older, and a lot more cynical."

He chuckled. "Lock the door and use that chain." It wasn't going to stop Talib from getting in if he tried, but it would give either Phoenix or Harbinger more time to respond. He stepped out and made sure not to touch the tiles that held the pressure plate. He stood outside the door until he heard the deadbolt turn and the chain slide into its slot. He exited the building the same way he'd entered and ghosted down the alley, leaving as an early morning bus passed the entrance in case anyone was watching from across the street. Pulling out his cell, he activated his earpiece app.

"This is Operator Two-Seven-Four. What can I do for you, Shadow Operative Fourteen?"

"You may resume surveillance."

"Of course. Anything else?"

"Nope, I'm good. Have a good day."

The operator chuckled, which was new. "Thank you. May your day go well. Operator Two-Seven-Four clear."

He locked his screen and shoved the phone back into his jeans. To make sure he wasn't being tracked or trailed, he wound his way through the inner city. About thirty minutes later, he entered a small establishment on the other side of the city center and took the booth at the very back. He ordered a coffee and breakfast because damn it, he was hungry.

The small bell above the door tinkled when he was halfway through his cup of coffee. He leaned back and watched the man stroll through the cafe. Harbinger was six feet, six inches tall, as lethal as they come, and one hell of an asset to have on your six.

He slid into the booth and waved over the waiter.

Harbinger ordered the same thing Reaper had ordered minutes earlier.

"What brings you around?" Reaper asked as he sipped his coffee.

"You took my job last night."

Reaper narrowed his eyes at the smirk on Harbinger's face. "She's mine."

Harbinger laughed at that and leaned back as the waiter brought his coffee and refilled Reaper's cup. "I'm not making a move on her, idiot. How long are we expecting this op to go?"

"At least thirty days."

"And thirty nights with you there?"

Reaper nodded. "Whenever I can. Why?"

"Just wondering why I'm in the country." The guy chuckled and sipped his coffee. "Bosses don't know you're in the apartment, do they?"

"Is it any of their concern?" Reaper leaned forward and lifted an eyebrow.

"Probably, but I'm just yanking your chain. Phoenix is watching her now. These two assholes that are threatening her, can't we just hunt them down and take them out?" Harbinger whispered the last question.

"I wish. Right now, Harmony may be the linchpin to getting information that will link two primaries in another operation."

"How so?"

"God, I wish we knew." Reaper saw the waiter approaching and leaned back. The tray was full of croissants, cheese, meat, jams, and whipped cream. They both dug into the food and ate before Reaper finished his thought. They were still the only people in the little cafe and the waiter was in the kitchen. He leaned in. "You've been briefed in." It wasn't a question, but Harbinger nodded anyway. "Behar Senior has slipped out of every accusation or charge lobbed his way. He always has layers of people beneath him that take the fall for anything he can't buy himself out of. Ardan is the same, but we finally have evidence that the Council acted on. Behar has been on Guardian's radar for the last couple of years. Those auctions put Behar Jr. and Ardan at the same place. If we can figure out the bidding, Behar wouldn't be able to wiggle out of the accusations."

Harbinger slathered cream onto another croissant and spooned some strawberry jelly on top of that. "Why not go after the auctioneer from the last auction? He should know what was being bid on."

"He's poofed." Reaper loaded up his pastry the same way Harbinger had.

"Really?"

"Anubis said the facial recognition program identified him, but no one has seen him since the auction."

"Dead," Harbinger mumbled through a mouthful of food.

"My bet."

"So, we wait until the next auction."

"And Harmony is our conduit to the working underlings, so we'll know if the auction is moved or changed in any way. I've got a tenuous connection with Behar Junior, so I'll work getting another invite through him. That's one sick fuck, let me tell you."

"Read his file. Too bad he's not coded. There is BDSM and then there's torture." His friend took a gulp of his coffee. "Speaking of torture, Phoenix isn't eating."

"Shit." Reaper stared down at his food. As a community, they kept an eye on the guy. He was the best at what he did. Unfortunately, what he did took a toll. Phoenix had confirmed it wasn't the things he did to extract information but the smell he recalled that stopped him from wanting to eat. "I'll see what I can do tonight. What time are you relieving him?"

"Dinner time, now." Harbinger winked at him.

"Thanks. I'll pick up some things and we'll hope for the best."

"It's all we can do. He's more open with you."

"We share some history."

"The Venezuelan mission." Harbinger nodded. "Lucky you had each other there."

Reaper grunted. "It was luck and then some." The mission had nearly killed them both, but they'd made it out. Barely. It took two months of healing, debriefing, and evaluation before either of them was allowed back into the field.

"The doc and his wife on the Mercy Team are here if you need to call them in." Harbinger lifted his eyebrow and stared at him.

"Man, I don't want to have to pull in the back office. How long has he been without food?"

"I saw him eat a sandwich the first day we did the recon and set up surveillance. Nothing since then. Speaking of her surveillance, there are two people who switch off during the day. Sometimes one, sometimes both, and never in the same place. They rotate and shift."

"Professional then?"

"Yeah, someone is paying to make sure that woman doesn't leave the building."

Talib, no doubt. His future plans for Harmony were personal and probably professional as Ardan would no doubt owe him if he delivered Harmony. "What about at night?"

"One in a car directly across from the front of her building. I take it you were able to unseal the back door?"

"I was."

"I'll slip in today and make sure there isn't any indication that you've managed to open it. Paint chips and shit that you might have missed in the dark."

"Appreciate it. We should be good. I double-checked."

"I'm bored, and it doesn't hurt to look at things in the daylight." Harbinger leaned back as the waiter started their direction. The waiter cleared the table and refilled their cups. Reaper took another sip. "We have an update in three hours. I have some recon to do before that."

Harbinger's eyes lit up. "Recon? Need help?"

Reaper chuckled. "I thought you'd never ask."

Reaper looked up as Harbinger dropped into the chair across from him. "That sick fucker. Do you know what he has in that small apartment?"

"A dungeon?" He didn't doubt it for a second.

"Practically, yeah. The son of a bitch has a cage with shackles. That's the only place that his women would stay because every other inch of that apartment is tools of his trade if you get me. I've hunted down serial killers. This guy is one murder away from dropping over the ledge."

The phone rang and both men leaned forward. Reaper answered it.

"Stand by, Sunset Operative Fourteen."

"Inform the Annex Sunset Operative Seventeen is present."

"Affirmative, stand by."

Harbinger looked up from the phone and whispered, "How did she vary?"

"I have no freaking clue." That was his standard answer when it came to Guardian's Operator. She was legendary and almost like an omniscient presence.

"Annex is on. Thirteen is on and authenticated. CCS will be joining us momentarily. Fourteen, authenticate Shallow."

"Grave."

"Seventeen, authenticate Portent."

"Herald." The man replied immediately. Reaper watched the phone as his friend authenticated his safety. Harbinger *was* the messenger of death. He heralded the passage of only the worst of the worst.

"We have recovered the body of the auctioneer from Cannes. It washed up on a beach in the south of France. It had been weighted and submerged. Drowning is the official cause."

"Ardan?" Reaper interjected.

"I doubt it." That was Val's voice. "He was with me the night of the auction. Did the body have clothes on?"

"The remains of a suit. Dark blue."

"Which was what the man was wearing the night of the auction," Reaper acknowledged. "It couldn't be Talib, we have the micro-RF on him."

"Who else would benefit from the auctioneer dying?" Harbinger asked.

"Behar Senior." CCS' voice cracked through the connection. "His yacht sailed to Cannes when the auction ended. The ship returned the next morning before dawn. Only twenty-point-eight-six miles away."

"Any witnesses or proof that Behar was on board?"

"Nope, but there is footage of a skiff with the auctioneer leaving the harbor. The video had to be enhanced and it was night, but for the short time he was under the lights, we confirmed he was alive. The men with him never looked up. No possibility of identification and none were the build or approximate age of Behar Senior." The clacking of a keyboard accompanied her voice.

"Thank you. Anything else?" Anubis asked.

"No, you got anything for me?" The woman returned the question.

"I do," Reaper answered. "Talib has indicated that he's gotten away with murder. Literally. Harbinger reconned the small apartment he owns. I checked out the other apartment, not his primary residence."

"There is a torture station in the small apartment. It is a lot more than a BDSM dungeon," Harbinger added.

"Can you look for any unsolved murders of females who had shackle marks on their arms and legs?" Reaper looked up at Harbinger who nodded.

"I can and I will. Paris location only?" she asked as the keys clacked away in the background.

"Does he own apartments in other cities?" Val asked.

"Yepper. New York, Paris, London, and Madrid."

"All of them," Reaper, Val, and Harbinger said at the same time.

"I gotcha. Let's see if we can connect the dots to

this nasty piece of human refuse. I'm warning you; it's going to take a hot minute, we're slammed. What priority is this?"

"Routine," Anubis replied, and Reaper cussed under his breath. He got it. Talib was small potatoes compared to his father and Ardan, but the fucker was still evil.

"Roger that. CCS out."

Anubis' voice filled the void. "Mercy Team is in Paris and on standby. As a last-ditch effort, should we not be able to figure out what the bidding means on auction night, we are going to interrogate one of the attendees before they make it to the auction. Should this happen, the plan would be for Fifteen to acquire one of the bidders. Fourteen, you would rendezvous with him and with Seventeen when you clear the auction and the artist is safe. Answers are paramount. We'll send vials to assist in questioning. However, if answers are not forthcoming, Fifteen is authorized to make them talk."

Shit. Phoenix wasn't eating now; burning the skin off another person wouldn't help the situation. He prayed the drugs would work. "We copy and understand all."

"Talib is on the move. We're tracking him via the RF chip. Any useful information will be sent to each of you. Thirteen, what is the status of your primary?"

"Status quo. No change. He's protected at all times; however, I have devised a plan should we be cleared to act prior to the auction."

"Understood. Do you need assistance for extraction?"

"Negative. I'm going to walk out the front door."

"I'll inform the hierarchy. Until we receive further information, we are on hold. Continue gathering any information you can. Annex out."

Reaper slid his finger over the face of the phone.

"That was a good call on Talib. He has to have left a string of bodies." Harbinger stood.

"If CCS can find something, it would help." Reaper nodded and stood too. "Let me know when you've relieved Phoenix."

"Will do. I'm going to hit the rack for a couple hours so I can stay up until you get to the apartment. You know these three-hour workdays are killing me."

Reaper snapped out a fist and punched Harbinger in the shoulder. The man laughed, avoided the next one, and was out the door before Reaper could reach him. Harbinger's laughter echoed in the hall of the hotel where Reaper was staying. Reaper pocketed his phone and grabbed his wallet. He needed to buy a few things for Phoenix and then, when it was dark, he was heading back to his Harmony. A smile lifted the corners of his lips as he remembered her in bed with the morning sun behind her. She was his angel.

Phoenix turned at the knock on his door. Harbinger's text hit at almost the same time.

> *I have the watchers. Answer the door.*

He got up and walked over to the door, his weapon in his hand as he answered it. Seeing Reaper and the items in his hands, he shook his head. "He should mind his own business."

"He is. We watch out for each other." Reaper elbowed into the apartment. "We need cups."

"I can do this myself." He watched his friend pull a bottle of bourbon out of the brown paper bag.

"Then why haven't you?" Reaper's eyebrow shot up.

Phoenix had no idea. Perhaps he was punishing himself like the shrinks at Guardian had suggested. "I'll get the cups."

By the time he was back, Reaper had everything

out of the other bags. Saltine crackers, cream cheese, and cooked chicken. Sometimes he could stomach more, most times he couldn't, but these three had usually worked.

Reaper poured a three-finger slug of bourbon and handed it to him. "Where's your head?"

Phoenix shrugged. "Same place it usually goes when I'm working alone."

"Which is why you need to consider working on a Thorn Team. At least then you'd have a partner."

Reaper took a sip of his drink and Phoenix downed half of his. When the burning in his throat passed, he shook his head. "It's bad enough that I see what I do to them. No one else needs to witness it."

"Then you need to talk to more than just me. What about Smoke?"

Phoenix huffed out a lungful of air. "He's got his hands full."

Reaper laughed. "Yeah, that hellion does keep him busy." He got serious and leaned forward. "You need someone else. What happens if I'm halfway around the world?"

"Like I said, I can do this." He waved at the food. He could, but damn it, he hadn't. There was something in his brain that prevented him from breaking his fast once he stopped eating. The smell is what triggered it. It could be just a whiff of smoke or exhaust or... anything that brought the stench of burning flesh into his mind. Not of his victims. No, the smell was from that first time. He closed his eyes.

"Drink and then try to eat one of these crackers." Reaper pulled him from his spiral. He did as his friend requested. Having nothing in his stomach, the bourbon worked fast. That was needed, too. Once he slept, he'd wake up and be ravenous.

"You're right. I need someone else in my life."

"Like a woman?" Reaper lifted his eyebrows a couple times.

"Not in a position to meet anyone, am I?" Phoenix finished his bourbon and took another cracker, one that Reaper had smeared with cream cheese.

"You never know. Think about the first class. Most of them are married or with someone permanent now."

"Yeah, but they're freaking dinosaurs." Phoenix carefully ate the cracker.

"Call Fury a dinosaur to his face," Reaper taunted him.

"Hey, I may have issues, but I'm *not* suicidal." Phoenix leaned back in the chair. "Thanks, man."

"Thank Harbinger. He told me. You got this

now?" Reaper handed him another cracker; this one had chicken on it.

"Why can't I just do it?" He snapped his mouth shut. Damn it, the bourbon was strong. He hadn't intended to say that out loud.

"It's a mental thing. Work with the shrinks and tell someone else. We've figured it out. It's a trust thing. You trust me. Who else?"

Phoenix stared at him. *No one.* At least not to the level he trusted Reaper.

"You need to let someone else get close, my friend. I think trust is the key. You trust me, know I'm not going to fuck you up. You need to let someone else as close to you as I am." Reaper leaned back and took a sip of his drink.

"I got no one, man." Phoenix leaned forward and grabbed another cracker.

"You've got me. You know I'm here for you, whatever it takes." Reaper lifted his cup in a toast.

Phoenix poured himself another healthy amount and lifted his cup, "As long as it takes, brother."

Reaper took a sip and pointed at him. "Don't ever forget that. I've got your back for as long as it takes. I'm not leaving. You couldn't make me. I'm just worried."

Phoenix nodded. "Thank you." Reaper stared at

him a minute, assumedly to make sure he understood. He did. They had each other's backs, and for that, he would be eternally grateful. He took another sip and accepted a small cracker from his friend. Reaper was right—what if his friend couldn't help? He did need someone else to be able to rely on. But who?

CHAPTER 16

Reaper glanced at his watch again. The sun was down. Just a few more minutes to make sure he hadn't been followed or tracked. He pushed back against the white plaster across the alley from Harmony's building. Over the course of the last three weeks, he'd made it up to her little apartment eighteen nights.

Three of those nights were spent drinking with Talib. The man had apologized profusely for passing out on him in Cannes and promised to show him Paris. The underbelly of Paris, that was. The places Talib frequented were not on the maps for tourists. Underground establishments that catered to the debauched acts of sadistic-minded bastards like Talib. The micro-RF chip had died; the trackers were only good for a week or so, but he'd gotten a good sense of a day in the life of Talib Behar. Those were times he'd like to scrub from his brain, which was saying something. Working for Guardian as an assassin, he'd seen things that he'd always carry with him. Talib's little tour was one of those items. He prayed Guardian could connect the man to the murders he claimed to have committed. Rotting in jail was too good for the man, but at least he'd be off the streets.

He spoke, "Operator, are you there?"

"I'm always listening. Do you need something?"

"You can take a break. I've got her."

"Affirmative. And thank you."

He jerked in the darkness. "For what?"

"Remembering to relieve me. Last night was…"

"Oh, shit." He'd brought edible paints to Harmony's apartment. They used them. All of them. Hadn't he… shit, no, he hadn't. "Why didn't you say something this morning when I told you to start monitoring again?"

"I'm chalking that up to shell shock," the operator quipped.

It was all he could do not to laugh out loud. "Duly noted. For future reference, you can stop listening when I enter the apartment."

"No, sorry. I must follow protocol and I can't be relieved unless you or another operative relieves me or the mission is terminated. But, as I have been relieved tonight, I bid you a good night. Operator Two-Seven-Four is clear."

Reaper rolled his eyes to the heavens and shook his head. Damn good thing he didn't embarrass easily. He moved silently across the alley and opened the door to the building, slipping through. Once in the stairwell, he took out his phone and connected directly to Harmony's earpiece. He clicked his fingers twice as he turned the corner to her floor. Her door opened, and she smiled at him. He carefully moved over the tiles and entered her apartment. She was in his arms before the door was shut.

"I missed you." She took his hand and pulled him into her studio. "Come, look, it's done."

He followed her. "The painting for LaVette?"

She looked back at him as she opened the studio door. "No, better." She dropped his hand and turned on the overhead light. The master she was working on looked complete, but there was a second easel set up without a canvas on it. "Hold on." She went to the stack of canvases standing upright in the room and reached in about midway. She pulled out the frame and held it away from him until she was at the easel. "This."

He blinked as he looked at the painting… of him. "When did you do this?"

"When I didn't feel like doing that." She scrunched her nose at the beautiful work of art on the first easel.

Reaper wasn't looking at the reproduction either. His eyes drifted over the portrait she'd done of him. The resemblance was uncanny, perfect, and painted with a loving hand. "It's fantastic." He stepped forward and stared at the canvas.

"I used some of the techniques I learned here, believe it or not. See here how the light seems to be the first thing that catches your eye, and then there's you? I worked on the shading first, which allowed me to get your features to pop. Then I used a fine three-hair brush to do your hair."

He stared at it, shaking his head. "It's like a photograph, but… damn, so much better."

"You like it?" She shoved her thumbnail between her teeth and stared at the canvas. "I could have done the relief better."

He turned to her and enfolded her into his arms. "You couldn't have done better. If this is how you see me, then I'm the luckiest man alive."

"Only because I'm the luckiest woman alive." She toed up and gave him a quick kiss. "You have to take it with you in the morning. Bernard was here this morning. He almost caught me looking at it. Thank goodness for that chain on the door."

"It will leave with me, but you shouldn't have risked painting it." He threaded his fingers through her hair as he spoke to her.

She shook her head and smiled. "You don't understand, I *had* to paint it. It wasn't a lark. Sometimes I see something and there is nothing I can do *but* paint what I see. When I saw you in Cannes and after I talked to you that first night, it was impossible to deny my muse."

"Thank you, my beautiful angel." He lowered and rubbed his lips against hers. Slowly, she melted against him, and he tightened his hold.

"We both know I'm not an angel."

"To me, you are." He bent and picked her up, carrying her to that small bed and the heaven that awaited them.

When he let her down, she reached for the hem of his t-shirt and shoved it up his chest. He obliged her and removed it, dropping it at the foot of the bed at the same time as he toed out of his shoes. They came together, and he kissed her with an all-consuming need. Her hands unfastened his belt, and he felt it the second the garrote snapped free from the buckle. He reached between them and moved her hands, unfastening his jeans, dropping them to the floor. He kicked out of his jeans and moved her away from his weapon. He killed with his hands when he was on an op with a knife and a garrote; the garrote he could conceal from Harmony, the knife he couldn't.

Harmony started to remove her clothes, and he helped. Working together, they were gone in mere moments. She surprised him by reaching back and grabbing a pillow from the bed. She dropped it in front of him and knelt down. Surprised, he carefully and softly placed his hands on her head. She'd rarely gone down on him when they were younger, so he didn't expect she would now.

She looked up at him, her big eyes serious. "I'm not good at this. I want you to tell me, to show me what feels good for you."

"I swear, anything you do will be perfect." His cock strained toward her. She could lick him like a lollipop and he'd explode. Warmth from her rapid exhale brushed over the sensitive skin of his cock. She leaned forward and kissed the tip of his shaft before she swirled her tongue around the head.

Instinctively, he wanted to clutch at her hair but forced himself to keep his grip reassuring, not threatening. She licked the underside of his cock with short, flicking swipes of her tongue.

He dropped his head back between his shoulder blades and stared at the ceiling. Excruciatingly sweet torture caused his thighs to tremble. At the feel of her nuzzling his balls, his eyes rolled into the back of his head. Not good at this? Who the hell told her that? She gripped the base of his shaft with her hand and sucked his cock into her wet, warm mouth. She gagged a bit as his shaft hit her soft palate. He tried to pull back, but her free hand wrapped around his thigh, keeping him where he was, which was more than okay with him. She pumped with her hand and met the upward stroke with the downward suction of her lips. The perfect sensation drew him closer to losing it. Damn it, he wanted this to last forever, but what she was doing to him wasn't going to let that happen. Then, her tongue flattened under his cock and rubbed every sensitive nerve ending with a hot velvet pull and drag as she lifted and lowered. He dropped his head and watched as his cock filled her mouth over and over. The visual pulled him so close to that unescapable edge. "Close." He gripped her hair a bit tighter when he spoke. Her hand tightened on his leg, and he understood what she wanted. He closed his eyes momentarily and then opened them wide. He wanted to see her when he...

His climax hit and he bent forward, holding her in position. That wonderful tongue worked against his cock, siphoning everything he had. Stuttering in a natural reaction, his hips moved forward, and she gagged. He pulled away only to have her chase him with her mouth. When he finished, she slowly released his shaft. Oversensitive, he shivered. Harmony stood up and took his hand, leading him to the bed.

He dropped down and pulled her to him. "Give me a second and I'll show you how much I enjoyed that."

She chuckled and snuggled close to him. "Take your time. I'm not going anywhere."

He wrapped her in his arms and drew a deep breath. "I wouldn't let you."

She tipped her head to see him. "I'm almost done with the auction piece. A few more layers in the upper right corner."

He stared at her, aided by the light in the studio that he hadn't bothered to turn off when he carried her out. "You're afraid."

She nodded. "I know you have people watching me, but I know Talib. He's been far too quiet."

He tightened his hold on her and let her tuck her head against his chest again. "I will kill him if he hurts you." That was a solemn vow. Off the books and alone, he'd hunt the bastard down and pull his intestines out and watch the man rot to death. A slow, painful death he could guarantee.

She chuckled. "I know you're exaggerating, but I get it. Thank you."

He held her and stroked her hair. Her breathing steadied out, and before long, she was asleep beside him. Six days until the auction, and then they'd be free of that bastard Talib. He stared at the wall, reaffirmed his vow, and considered just how he was going to make the man suffer if he ever touched Harmony again.

CHAPTER 17

R eaper glanced down the pedestrian-crowded street from the terrace of a rooftop bistro on Rue Joseph de Maistre in Montmartre. Harbinger would meet him here, and together they were going to tail the messenger that at this moment was having lunch two tables down from him. If Phoenix was needed, they'd call someone in to relieve him from watching Harmony's apartment.

Inside the messenger's pouch were the invitations to the auction. No one knew the location, contrary to the event in Cannes. What he did know was Talib was personally delivering the invitations to the messenger company. Following that pompous idiot amounted to child's play.

Talib had steadfastly refused to divulge the informa-

tion. "My instructions are exact. I cannot release that information because I won't know until a couple hours before the rest of you. But be assured, you will have the invitation in time to arrange for transportation, that I promise you."

"Why such mystery this time?"

Talib gave a huff and waved in the air with the hand not holding his scotch. "The stakes are bigger this time."

"You mean the bidders are richer?" He took a sip of his scotch. The company he was currently with turned the exquisite taste of the expensive liquor into turpentine.

Talib looked at him and lifted an eyebrow. "That is not what I mean." He shrugged. "But let's not talk about the auction. Afterward, I will have a tasty treat all to myself. I have secured this delicacy at quite an expense and after much hardship, but it is done. After the auction, I must meet with others for a brief period. You should wait and then help me break in my newest project."

Reaper took a sip of the sparkling water he'd ordered and pondered Talib's words. Once he and Harbinger interrogated one of the bidders with the help of chemicals, they should know everything that Guardian would need to know to go to the Council. He swirled the water and glanced down to the street below.

Harbinger pulled up on a motorcycle and parked

the bike across from the restaurant. "In position." Harbinger's words were loud and clear in his earpiece. He wouldn't acknowledge the communication; it wasn't necessary.

He finished the food he'd ordered while the messenger finished his meal and two glasses of wine. The man paid for his food after Reaper had, so following him out of the building was an act of coincidence. The messenger turned right out of the main doors of the hotel where the restaurant was located. Reaper turned left. "Black shirt, blue jeans, messenger bag." He described Harbinger's bogey as he made his way to his nondescript rental car.

"On him," was Harbinger's reply.

Reaper turned on his car, rolled down his window, and waited.

"Heading down Rue Joseph de Maistre toward Rue Caulaincourt." Harbinger's voice vibrated from the ride on his motorcycle.

"Copy." He pulled out into traffic and made his way after Harbinger. "Turning right on Rue Caulaincort."

"Affirm."

He followed suit, and when he was able, he sped up and then caught up with Harbinger. "Roll through the roundabout in a three-sixty. I'll lead."

"Copy." He had the messenger's motorcycle in his sights when Harbinger peeled off and used the roundabout to end up following. He'd drop back so the messenger wouldn't see him.

"We're on Boulevard de Clinchy," Reaper spoke as he drove. "There is another roundabout. Take the lead."

Harbinger passed him, and he decelerated, drifting back. They drove for a few minutes before he heard Harbinger's words.

"Second exit onto Place de Clinchy, then onto Boulevard des Batingnolles."

They tag-teamed the messenger through the city onto Avenue de Wagram and around the round-about at the Arc de Triomphe. He was leading and echoed his driving directions to Harbinger. "Fifth exit onto Avenue Kléber."

"He's heading to 16th Arrondissement," Harbinger said as Reaper let him pass.

"One of the richest neighborhoods in Paris. Makes sense," Reaper agreed.

"Large international community, also." Harbinger didn't say anything as they continued the dance of following the messenger and then he chirped, "And if you look to your left, ladies and gentlemen, you can see the spire of the Tour Eiffel."

"I've had the nickel tour, thank you."

"I can tell you how long the Seine is."

"No, thanks. Watch out, he's slowing down. You take this, I'm going past and parking out of sight. We'll watch for the best chance to not be seen."

"On it."

They followed the messenger as he delivered nine different invitations, the last of which Reaper mentally tagged. It was a residence, not an apartment. There were gardens surrounding the house and no risk of being seen should they need to force their way in.

"That one," Harbinger said as he drove past Reaper who was parked along the side of the road.

"I agree. Park and make your way back. I'll check for an alarm system."

"Copy."

Reaper got out of his vehicle and strolled past the house. After making sure there was no one else to see him disappear, he slipped into the thick stand of shrubbery and quietly made his way to the rear of the house. He pulled out a pair of high-powered binoculars and focused on the windows.

High-tech sensors were placed on the sides of the windows. So, he'd need to find the... *Ah, there.* He studied the communications lines which were housed in a metal casing. A ninety-degree turn into the house was where he'd be able to access the wires.

He assessed the backyard and the windows at the rear of the residence. No movement. He pocketed his small binoculars and jogged across the yard. He strong-armed the ninety-degree metal angle away from the building. A smile split his lips. The tech inside the house was new and sophisticated; however, the Parisian infrastructure wasn't. He stripped the wire he needed and bypassed the comms and alarm.

"Copper?" Harbinger's question reverberated in his ear.

He nodded, knowing his partner was watching him. "Backdoor."

"En route."

He finished his work and made his way to the door where he met Harbinger. With practiced ease, they entered the unlocked door. They shut it behind them and listened to the movements of the residence. There wasn't any sound. The kitchen was pristine and unused. Reaper nodded, and Harbinger followed him. They made their way to the front of the house. Harbinger tapped him on the arm and pointed toward an open door. He nodded. They moved forward.

Their target worked on his laptop, facing the wall, not the door. Idiot. Reaper reached into his pocket and withdrew a syringe. He pulled the cap silently. Harbinger grabbed the man and shot him full of drugs.

The man's startled shout died out, but Reaper had spun around and waited for anyone coming to the man's aid. There was no one. "I'm going to check to make sure."

"No problem. I'll stay here with our pincushion." Harbinger spun the man's chair and tapped his cheek with his hand. "He's down, but we need to give the chemicals some time to work."

"I'll be back. Don't start the fun without me." It took less than five minutes to clear the entire residence. He jogged down the stairs and into the room where Harbinger and the man were waiting.

"Ready?"

"Hold on." Reaper pulled out his phone and accessed the direct link app for their earpieces. He added Val, Anubis, and CCS. They authenticated and were given the go to proceed with the questioning from Anubis.

"What is your name?" Harbinger asked in French.

"Louis Detreau. Who are you?" The man's eyes closed. "I don't feel well."

"What are you buying at the auction?" Reaper asked the question as Harbinger fixed the final syringe they would give the man.

"Weapons."

"How do you do that?" Reaper asked again.

"Bid on the painting to the right or the left of the main artwork."

"Is there a difference between the right and the left artwork?" Reaper snapped the question.

"Right are small arms, set fee. Left is heavy weapons. The type varies at each auction. So does the price."

"Good. Now tell me what you get if you bid on the main art?"

"War. A coup, enough men and the weapons to overthrow a government."

"Who provides the weapons?" Reaper held the man's eyes.

"Ardan. I'm going to be sick."

"You'll be fine in a minute. Who arranges the effort to overthrow the government?"

"Talib Behar and Ardan."

"Talib?" Both he and Harbinger said at the same time.

"Yes."

Reaper leaned forward. "Not his father?"

The man frowned and shook his head. "His father is dead."

"When did he die?"

"Last year, maybe before."

"How?"

"Talib killed him."

CCS chimed in. "On it."

"Do you pay at the auction for your weapons?"

"Half, a wire transfer. Half on arrival, cash." The man gagged and moaned, "Who are you? What's happening?"

Anubis came online. "All right. Give him the final vial. I'll take this to Archangel. We are status quo until orders change. Fourteen, your primary is Senior until we verify he's out of the picture. Thirteen, you're still on Ardan. Seventeen, stay with this guy to make sure anyone else in his party doesn't suspect anything. We're too close to have a stray memory fuck this up."

"Affirm," Reaper answered, his mind traveling faster than his words over the comm devices. *Talib?* The bastard was either an excellent actor or Louis had his information wrong. He had to have his information wrong. "Talib knew nothing when I drugged him."

"We all know there are countermeasures to the drugs," Anubis replied.

"That would mean he's on to me," Reaper thought out loud while Harbinger injected their hostage. "And the invite for after the auction would be a trap."

"CCS, how close are you to verifying what our unwilling informant provided?"

Bengal's voice came over the comms. "She's working it. I'll let you know as soon as she confirms or disproves the intel."

"Roger that. Everyone has their orders. The auction may use wi-fi to access those transactions. Thirteen, as soon as you get the location, inform CCS. I want to be able to trace the money."

"Affirm."

He repeated his acknowledgement and stared at Louis who was, at the moment, sleeping. Soon, he'd be huddled over a toilet with the worst flu known to man and no memory of what had happened this afternoon.

"Help me." Harbinger grabbed one of Louis' arms and Reaper grabbed the other. "Hard to believe that Talib could be our ringmaster," Harbinger grunted as they moved the dead weight into the bathroom.

"The sadistic bastard is sick enough to murder his old man." Reaper had no doubt on that point.

"Okay, I've got it from here. I'll wipe the house and wait to make sure any friends of his find him and there isn't any concern other than for his health."

"Whatever it takes." Reaper headed toward the door.

"As long as it takes, brother." Harbinger finished the statement.

Harmony placed her easel in the front room and then brought out the copy that she'd been working on. The 3D photographs she'd been given for each work of art had allowed her to copy each painting in a detail she wouldn't be able to do otherwise. This work of art was in a museum. She stared at the painting and the photo in her hand. How had they gotten this close to the real work of art? How had they been able to manipulate it so she could see the brushstrokes from every angle? She studied the photograph, or rather, the background of the photo. Pulling another from the stack, she gazed at it, and then another, and another. *A vault?* There were shelves made of some type of thick metal. *A walk-in*

safe? She stared at the background. Documents and other boxes lined the shelves. What caught her attention was a rack where other frames were stacked standing up, and a few were draped in dust cloths.

Was she copying a copy? She closed her eyes and pinched the inside corners. Who really cared? This time tomorrow, she and Roman would be flying out of Paris. He'd promised her that he'd come for her in the morning. His responsibility tonight was to his employer. Which, to be truthful, sucked. She'd hoped she'd be done with this place as soon as she turned over the painting, that Roman would walk in after Bernard walked out. Foolish. The auction was important for reasons Roman couldn't go into. It didn't matter; all of this was almost done.

She sighed and rubbed the back of her neck and then glanced at the battery-operated clock above the kitchen sink. Bernard would be here shortly. Thank God she wasn't required to be dangled in front of their bosses again.

A knock on her door startled her even though she was expecting Bernard. She answered the door, leaving the chain in place. Bernard lifted an eyebrow at her, and she closed the door, removing the chain and opening the door.

Bernard walked past her straight to the canvas, propping the leather carrying case at the foot of the easel. He put on a pair of glasses and leaned over the art. She was used to his intense study of her work. "Excellent. You dried it according to specifications."

"Yes I did, and thank you. What am I doing next?" She sat on the arm of the couch as he carefully placed the painting into the carrying case.

"I'm not sure. I'll let you know." Bernard zipped the case and headed toward the door.

"What am I supposed to do until then?"

Bernard turned at the door. "If you want to live? Follow instructions." He opened the door and walked out, shutting it behind him.

She smiled at the closed door. That would be the last she'd see of Bernard. Tonight, she'd have a glass of wine and try to sleep. Jolting at another knock at the door, she glanced at the chain that she hadn't resecured. She put her foot against the door and opened it a bit. A shoulder pushed the door open, and a wet rag was shoved over her face. She shook her head wildly, trying to say something that would let the operator know she was in trouble, but Talib's firm grip over her mouth prevented anything but a muffled gasp. She knew she was going to pass out. With her last vestige of strength, she raked her fingernails across his face. He pulled away and she inhaled, but his fist collided with her jaw before she could speak. Her head hit the floor; the whack of the sound reverberated through her skull as blackness overtook her.

CHAPTER 18

Phoenix cocked his head and watched as Bernard LaVette left the building with the carrying case, heavier now due to the way he was carrying it. The man entered the car that waited for him, and it drove away. He swept the street from the apartment he'd rented diagonal from Harmony's apartment. The watchers were there today. Both of them, which wasn't unusual. He took a sip of his water. Thanks to Reaper, he'd defeated his demons, at least for now, and was eating. He popped another cookie into his mouth and chomped down.

Movement caught his attention. One of the watchers stood and wandered down the block. He panned back to the other and tensed immediately when he saw the other leave. Palming his phone, he called in.

"Operator Two-Seven-Four."

"Send me to the Annex, Priority Dusk."

"Stand by."

"Annex. Go."

"The painting is gone, but so are the watchers."

"Explain."

"I can't. LaVette left, and three or four minutes later, the watchers peeled away. Both of them."

"Stand by, I'm patching into the operator."

"Operat—"

"What is the status of Harmony Flinn?"

"Stand by. Accessing." There was a brief pause. "Sir, I have the conversation with LaVette. A few muffled sounds, but no calls for help. Would you like me to contact her?"

"Yes."

"Ms. Flinn, are you okay?"

There was silence. The operator repeated herself, "Ms. Flinn, this is the operator. I need to know your status."

"Phoenix, get over there."

He was out the door before Anubis finished the statement. He sprinted down the stairs and out of his apartment building. On the street, he dodged pedestrians and was damn near hit by two different cars. Shouting drivers vilified his existence as he hurdled over trash cans that were chained to a streetlight on Harmony's side of the street.

Phoenix slammed into the front door of her apartment building and surged up the stairwell almost sideways because it was so damn tight. He took the stairs three at a time, and at the landing, swiped his automatic from his leg holster. He counted the apartments. The door to hers was standing wide open. He stepped over the plate-sensitive tiles into the apartment. A smudge of blood on the floorboard. He darted through the rest of the apartment to make sure she wasn't hiding, but... "She's gone. There's blood. A small amount on the floor just inside of the threshold."

"Operator, ping her via the earpiece locater." Anubis snapped the directive.

"I already have, sir. She's in the apartment."

Phoenix's eyes swept the wood floors. He saw it, halfway to the corner of the room. He walked over and picked up the small clear piece of plastic. "Her earpiece is here." Phoenix swore bitterly. "I promised him I'd watch over her."

"Stand by," Anubis commanded. "Operator, patch me through to CCS."

"CCS." Bengal's voice snapped through Phoenix's comms.

"Harmony Flinn has been taken. She doesn't have the earpiece." Anubis pushed the information as fast as he could. "Approximately seven minutes ago. I need access to street cameras, anything in the location that would capture a vehicle."

"She had to have left through the rear of the building. I was monitoring the front."

"Copy all. Stand by." Bengal's voice rang clear.

Phoenix flicked his wrist and looked at the time. *Fuck.* Reaper did not need this shit, not now. He was probably en route to the fucking auction by now. "It was coordinated. The watchers pulled away together. They knew when their services were no longer required." He walked to her small window and the view of the building across the alley. Damn it, he couldn't let this go. Harmony was Reaper's woman. That meant she was family. "She's family, Bengal." Anubis' comment echoed his thoughts. He put the tiny earpiece in his pocket and walked into the studio area of her apartment. There were several paintings, some completed, some not, that tilted against the wall. The woman had talent. Everything in the room was beautiful. Reaper was lucky that his woman saw such beauty.

Phoenix turned off the light and walked back into the small living area. He'd never have that in his life, but he wouldn't let some bastard take it from Reaper.

"We've got nothing. Not a damn thing." Bengal's voice growled out the words.

"Okay, primary suspect is Talib," Phoenix said as he jogged out of the tiny apartment. "How many residences does he have?"

Anubis was on the idea as quickly as he was. "Three. Harbinger did surveillance on one. Reaper took the other one, Talib is living in the third. Stand by."

Instead of turning left and going out the door at the bottom of the stairwell, he turned right and jogged to the back of the building. Damn it. The door stood wide open; smashed hardware told him that whoever opened the damn door didn't know it had been unsealed. He stopped at the threshold. Another drop of blood and… *yes, there.* He worked his way into the alley, then nothing. There had to be a vehicle here waiting.

"Harbinger's online."

"I would have been compromised if I answered sooner. The contingent with Louis has left one person to tend to him and left for the auction. I listened to the entire conversation. Louis told them the account number and the amount to bid and on which picture," Harbinger spoke quietly.

"Noted. Harmony Flinn was abducted."

"Fucking Talib." Harbinger spit out the words.

"It is our assumption. The apartment you did recon on, could he hold her there while he went to the auction?"

Harbinger sighed, "Yeah, he could. Depends on the auction site."

"Reaper indicated a new up and coming gallery in the Belleville region." Phoenix rattled off the address.

"That's at least two hours away through city traffic from the dungeon I saw."

"Dungeon?" Phoenix's stomach turned.

"Yeah, the man is into hurting his women. Long, drawn-out pain from the looks of the equipment he had stashed."

"Then that location is out. Phoenix, Harbinger, there are two remaining residences. CCS, get them the address they are closest to in order to save time. Talib will be at the auction, that starts in less than an hour."

"What about Reaper?" Phoenix popped the question as he looked at his phone and the incoming text with the address. He plugged it into his GPS and sprinted back to the rental car he had parked two blocks away.

"His head needs to stay in the game."

"What?" Harbinger's question was shouted so loud it rattled Phoenix's brain. "No way, Anubis, he has to know. Tell him we've got it. But I'm telling you, he has to know."

"I concur." Phoenix added his two cents.

"So do I." Bengal's voice was a surprise addition. "Reaper can keep his shit together. They need to know all the information you have. What if he uses Harmony to draw out Reaper? He needs to know."

"Granted, but I'm not telling him until he arrives at the auction. I can't have him going rogue. We are too damn close."

"Do we have a go yet?" Bengal asked the question Phoenix wasn't authorized to ask. Damn it, why hadn't the Council coded the bastards?

"Still waiting. Everyone has their assignments. Keep me informed. Annex out."

Phoenix slammed his car door shut and revved the engine. He had a long way to go. Damn it, he prayed Harmony was at one of the residences, that they could inform Reaper that she was safe. But something in his gut told him that wouldn't be the case.

∾

Reaper took in the converted industrial garage as he stepped inside. The dramatic showroom was quiet with the exception of a small contingent of people gathered around the side table and another small group that examined the three works of art in the middle of the empty space. He moved forward and snagged a glass of champagne from one of the waiters currently making their way through the small crowd.

He saw Val with Ardan and headed the opposite direction. His earpiece activated as he walked toward the paintings. "I have an update for you." Anubis came through loud and clear. He didn't acknowledge the comms. "Brace yourself and do not react." He stopped in front of a painting and slid his hand into his pocket. Whatever he had to say, Anubis was using caution so as not to pull him from his undercover work. "Harmony was taken from her apartment today. The bastard smashed through the back door, so he wasn't aware it had been opened."

He kept his eyes on the painting in front of him, but he couldn't see a damn thing except the brilliant red of rage. He drew a deep breath and let it out in slow increments. "Phoenix and Harbinger are going to each of Talib's residences. We'll find her."

He looked left and right. Completely alone, he replied. "The bastard's mine."

"He is." Anubis agreed. "The Council has coded Talib. CCS was able to confirm his father has not been seen by any security cameras in his casino for twenty months, six days."

He glanced around to make sure he was still alone. "How could no one notice?"

"If there was anyone who was brave enough, they were probably eliminated or bought off. Talib is coded. I'll let Thirteen know she's a go. Take him out, let us worry about Harmony. She's family. We'll find her."

He let his eyes drift left and right again. "She's my heart."

"I know. We'll do whatever it takes for as long as it takes to find her. Annex out."

He turned and stared at the painting he'd watched Harmony laboring over for the last month. Working to control the hatred and rage pounding through his veins, he took a long sip of the champagne and then set the glass on one of the waiters' trays. He moved closer to Val, who gave him a side-eyed glance. He dropped his eyes to her hand. She signed, "Stay the course."

He snorted to himself. He had zero desire to stay the fucking course. He wanted to slam Talib into the glass and metal sculpture at the front of the building and kill him slowly, but only after the bastard told him where Harmony was.

He cocked his head and ran with that thought. Talib was his to kill. His specialty didn't make things look like an accident or a natural passing. Reaper made himself wander through the exhibit that was opened near the three auctioned paintings. He made statements. His garrote made statements.

He glanced at his watch. Fucking time was not on his side. He did the mental math. For Anubis to have the information he had and to have dispatched both Harbinger and Phoenix, the notification to him had been delayed. Twenty or thirty minutes? He paused in front of a particularly hideous contemporary art painting and calculated the time to travel from Harmony's apartment to any of the three residences Talib had in the city. It would be almost impossible to take her to any of those locations and be here at a reasonable time to start the—

"Ah, there you are. Enjoying the art?" Talib walked up behind him.

"Some of the pieces. Some are dreadful." He turned to look at the bastard that he'd soon decapitate. A fresh set of fingernail scratches ran from the corner of his mouth down the side of his neck. "Someone get the better of you, my friend?"

"Oh, this? A hissing kitten. Tell me, have you considered my offer?"

"Offer?" Reaper was being purposefully obtuse as he silently cheered for Harmony. She'd marked the bastard.

"To come with me and taste the delights of my new plaything. Such a feisty one, this American."

Reaper cocked an eyebrow and shrugged. "I'm tired of Americans. They are, as you say, feisty. I prefer my playthings more compliant."

Talib blinked and snapped his eyes to Reaper. "She's very talented. An artist." Talib threw out more chum into the water, looking for a response, no doubt. *But why?*

Reaper sighed and lifted a finger for the waiter. He took two champagne flutes and handed one to Talib. "Are we going to watch her sculpt?"

Talib's eyes narrowed. "Paint."

"Ah, the little blonde you said you wanted. Congratulations on obtaining her." Reaper toasted Talib and took a sip.

"Yes, the very one. I plan on breaking her in tonight. Of course, she'll be branded and tattooed if she survives tonight. I'll pierce her so I can link chains through the piercings and walk her when or if I ever take her out of her cage."

"Sounds utterly enthralling," he drawled. "Do you watch as they brand your toys?"

"I do the branding. Electric branding iron specifically made for me." The bastard had the audacity to adjust himself. "And the pain I can inflict with a fresh brand is intoxicating."

"Pardon me." Bernard LaVette spoke, turning both of them. "The auction is about to begin."

"Oh, but of course. Excuse me, please? We will discuss this further tonight. Oui?"

"Oui," he agreed, and Talib beamed. He lingered by the horrid painting, speaking once he knew he was alone. "He didn't have time to take her to one of his residences."

"Copy. Working on it." Anubis answered him. "He's baiting you."

"The question is why? There is no tie between Harmony and me, none that he'd know about."

"Working on that, too," Anubis answered.

Reaper turned and made his way to the front of the gallery where bidders with their paddles awaited. He put on his glasses and pushed the rim, starting the recording of what he saw. The auctioneer stepped onto the platform. He glanced nervously toward Talib, who smiled broadly at the man.

"Ladies and gentlemen, today, we first offer the painting on my right, your left..." He described the painting and extolled the artist's gifts. He opened the bidding, and each bidder raised his card. Reaper kept Ardan in his sights. A slight nod toward the auctioneer's assistant was all it took. Four people bid on the small arms cache. There were two bidders for the larger weapons. When the auctioneer turned to the main attraction there were three bidders. This time, the bidding went on, each bidder trying to outbid the other. At one hundred million euros, one contingent fell out. The other two kept bidding. The winner of the coup bid one hundred seventy-seven million euros. Polite applause sounded around the room, but that wasn't what Reaper noticed. He noticed the terrified look the auctioneer sent Talib's way.

Talib was not happy.

Reaper made his way over to Talib. "Impressive price for the last piece."

"No. Not really. There was a minimum required bid, the auctioneer failed."

"Really? How much?"

"One hundred and eighty million euros."

"I can blow through three million in a weekend." Reaper snapped his fingers.

Talib's anger was palpable. "It is not a small sum. He failed to follow directions."

"What if he didn't sell the painting?"

"It would have gone on auction again."

Reaper sighed, "I guess it's time to get a new auctioneer."

"It would seem. Now, I must tend to business before we go on to the best part of the evening."

"But of course." He watched Talib walk toward Ardan and Val. She gave Talib an up-and-down look and dismissed him immediately. Reaper would have smiled if the situation was different.

"She's not in either of the closer residences."

He assumed that, but where would she be? "I'm going with him after the auction winds down. He said he had her. I'll ask to play. When I have her, I'll take him out."

There was silence for a long moment. "And if she sees and understands what you've done?"

"I'll deal with that when or if it happens." Saving

her was paramount. If she found out what he truly was, then so be it.

"Fifteen and Seventeen are en route. Seventeen will back up Thirteen, and Fifteen will be with you. Mercy Team is now at the center of the city."

"I won't need help, but keep Mercy Team on standby." He swallowed hard and forced the truth from his lips. "Talib may have already hurt her." Reaper leveled a stare at Talib. This man was a piece of human trash, and based on the Council's coding, was his to kill. If anything had happened to Harmony, it would be an immediate death for the man.

CHAPTER 19

R eaper got into the chauffeur-driven vehicle with Talib; the man's demeanor had turned sour as soon as the driver pulled into traffic. "If you aren't feeling like company, I don't mind."

Talib shook his head. "I had information provided to me that I doubted and now know to be untrue. I'm irritable. Forgive me. I'll take it out on my new plaything."

Reaper chuckled. "I have an idea tonight will be enjoyable." Assassinations were a duty to his country. He took no pleasure in death, but tonight, that rule would be broken. Tonight, he would watch the life drain out of the man beside him. "Where are we going?"

"Ah, I have a ship I rent berthed at Paris Port." Talib sighed. "What is your full name?"

"I've told you. Conrad Belmonte." He cocked his head at Talib. "Why?"

"Do you believe in doppelgangers?"

He frowned. "You mean people who look like each other? I suppose it could happen. Why?"

Talib waved a hand. "I research my playthings very carefully. No one to miss them when they are gone, yes?"

"They do tend to have a shelf life, don't they?" He wanted to puke, but he pulled off a smile.

"Indeed. In my research, they provided me a picture of this plaything's childhood sweetheart."

"So, when you say you do your research, you really meant it. Why in the hell would you want a picture of her boyfriend?" Reaper turned and tried his damnedest to look completely enthralled.

"I monitored her telephone calls. His name was mentioned. I felt it was a matter of necessity."

"Okay, so what about the picture?"

Talib stared at him. "He looks like you."

Reaper blinked and backed up a bit before he leaned forward. "May I see it?"

"Why would you want to?"

"Because I want to see my doppelganger.

Wouldn't you?" He laughed and slapped his thigh. "Can you imagine the mindfuck when you introduce me to your new toy?"

Talib seemed to relax. "Indeed, it could be very interesting."

"That's what gets me off, screwing with their mind. I want them to be at my mercy, not physically but mentally."

Talib chuckled. "For me, it's all about pain."

"I've noticed."

Talib jerked and narrowed his eyes. Reaper held up a hand and chuckled, "Not saying anything, my friend, we all have our own kink. Live and let live. Me, I'd treat the brand you spoke of as a mark of honor. Only the best of the best is marked by me. I'd make her beg for it and thank me after I do it." Acid rose in Reaper's throat as he talked. The thought of hurting a woman who was trusting you for care and love pierced through him like a diamond-tipped spear, but he had to keep it together for Harmony.

The car came to a stop, and Talib exited the vehicle. Reaper got out and walked with him.

"Fifteen is three minutes out and coming fast." Anubis' voice in his ear was the only sound besides the muted sounds of traffic.

"Which one?"

"Here." Talib pointed to a decrepit scow of a boat.

"This? Is it water worthy?"

Talib laughed as he walked up the gangplank. "It works for my needs." He took out a set of keys and unfastened four deadbolts. He pulled a side panel open and put in a code that Reaper couldn't see, but he heard the four beeps.

"Top-notch security for a rust bucket berthed in the middle of all these nice boats." The metal construction of the boat could hinder his earpiece, and he wanted Phoenix to have as much information as possible.

"Only the best," Talib agreed as he shoved the door open.

It wasn't a door, and this wasn't a ship. It was a fucking vault. They walked through the door and the cold, forced air met them. Talib flipped on a switch and LED lights illuminated the floor. He shut the vault door behind them and motioned for Reaper to follow. While they were walking in the semi-darkness, Reaper thumbed his belt buckle. His garrote was ready.

"What are all these doors?" There were four on each side.

"Playthings that are in various stages of training. Would you like to see?"

Reaper stopped. "Absolutely."

Talib turned. He pushed a button and the metal door lifted. Inside a ten-by-ten cage was a woman. Her hair had been chopped off and there were bloody spots on her scalp. She was terribly thin and curled in the corner, shivering. "This is one. It tried to take food off my plate. It was punished for it."

It? The fucker was going to die, but somehow that didn't seem enough. Reaper stared at the huddled woman in the corner of the cell. She didn't even look up. She was indeed broken.

"This one receives pain well, better than most. She still has a will to live. Soon, I'll break her of that, too. Then she'll be finished."

"How many do you have?"

"In this boat? Six on this level and my new one below."

"Do you have other boats?"

"No. I have places in the city that I'll take particularly interesting items when they learn what is required of them, but I kennel them here."

"Wise. So, the new one?" There would be no reason for the police to look at this boat. It was the perfect hiding place.

"Ah, yes, below. Come." Talib pushed the button, dropping the metal door on the poor caged woman.

He walked down the lighted path and opened another door at the end of the hallway. "Watch your step," Talib cautioned before he walked down the stairs.

Reaper glanced back at the six cages and mentally vowed to the women inside he'd help them. He hit the bottom of the stairs and was face to face with the business end of an automatic. He glanced at the nine mil and then at Talib. Nine mil to the brain or heart and he was dead; other than that, he had a fighting chance if the man was a shit shot. He slowly lifted his hands and asked, "What is this?"

"This is me making sure my tracks are covered. You mysteriously appear, attempt to make a friend of me, and use chemicals to try to get me to talk. If you are not Roman Alexander, you are someone who means to move on my business. Either way, you will die."

Reaper sighed heavily. "Of course, I'm trying to find out about your business. But I'm not like your little toys. I will be missed."

"Accidents happen all the time."

"Accidents with bullet holes in them? I think not," Reaper chuckled. "I could have killed you when I drugged you. I did not. I want a part of the business. I know Ardan. I know what he does. What you're doing with him, I'm not so sure, but like-minded businessmen are better bedfellows than you and that old man, wouldn't you agree? I have nearly unlimited finances, and after I figure out what you're doing, I'll be a silent partner. My thrills, like I said, are mental. I want in."

Talib laughed. "I have a fortune. What I'm doing now is taking over the world one country or organization at a time, and Ardan is expendable now. I am taking over everything. I will be the only one to profit. I don't do partners."

Reaper slipped from his cover persona. He settled his weight and exhaled, crouching a bit as he did. "Then pull the trigger. I'm not one of your playthings, Talib." Talib shot a glance toward the stairs where they'd entered. Reaper shook his head slowly and let a menacing smile slide across his face. "I don't need backup."

Talib's hand started to shake. So, the fucker wasn't as stupid as he looked. "Who are you?"

Lightning quick, Reaper struck Talib's hand. The gun fired in the confined area, the sound deafening. Reaper lunged, taking Talib to the ground. The man was quick and rolled to his left. Reaper moved to his right and was on his feet faster than Talib. Talib lunged for the weapon, but Reaper kicked the handgun behind him. To reach the gun, Talib would have to get past him. That would never happen.

A smile spread across Reaper's face. "You want to know who I am? I'm death, and I've been sent for you."

The man's lip curled into a snarl. "You can try to kill me. Many have."

Reaper stepped forward and Talib retreated. The man's eyes flicked to the right. Reaper wasn't going to be distracted. "The world's leaders have judged you guilty for killing your father."

Talib blinked, the surprise immediate. The man shook his head. "You can't prove it."

Reaper advanced again. Talib danced and backed up a step at the same time. Reaper laughed. "I don't have to. You've also been judged for providing mercenaries and weapons to overthrow governments, causing countless deaths and suffering."

Talib licked his lips. His eyes flicked to the right once more. "Again, no proof."

"Enough proof for the Council to code you for execution."

"And I assume you are the executioner?" Talib sneered.

"I *am* that executioner. My name is Reaper, and I will take you to hell where you belong."

"A Guardian." Talib spit the words at him.

"I am. The world has judged you, Talib Behar, and now it is time for you to die."

"Even if you kill me, you won't be able to stop what I've contributed to. Guardian's days are numbered. Never forget, I owe you." Talib shot a hand to the right, hitting a button. Lights illuminated a chamber.

Harmony hung from a St. Andrew's cross, blood covering the front of her shirt.

Talib used the distraction and lunged forward, tackling Reaper at the knees.

Reaper grappled with the smaller man as he fell to the metal floor. Talib was frantic and erratic in his punches and jabs, not mounting a strong defense or any kind of offense. Reaper raised his knee between them and lifted the smaller man from his body. He delivered a right hook, dropping Talib to the ground. Reaper stood and drew back his foot. With all the force he could muster, he kicked Talib in the ribs. Reaper sneered when the crack of bone and scream from the man echoed in the metal box. Talib groaned and rolled away. "That was for the women upstairs." Reaper followed him and stepped on his hand as he reached for the gun. "Shall I break you? Shall I make you beg? How much pain can you tolerate, you sadistic son of a bitch?" He fell on top of the man, keeping him on his belly. It took nothing to sling his garrote around Talib's neck. "You're lucky I can't take my time. But know this. You made my woman bleed. If she's seriously hurt, I will find you in hell and I will make the devil look like a fairy princess, you motherfucking bastard. This is for the woman I love. The woman you dared to touch. Rot in hell."

"Roman?"

Harmony's voice snapped his eyes to the cell that Talib had illuminated. She was still fully clothed; one side of her face was swollen three times the size it should be, and blood was caked under her nose and dried where it had flowed down her chin and chest. She stared down at him, beaten and abused.

He whispered, "I'm sorry you have to see this." He held her eyes as he snapped the garrote tight and beheaded the bastard under him.

Talib's head rolled about a foot. The spray of blood from his beating heart painted the metal wall. Reaper stood and walked over to the cage where she hung. Her hands were blue, the restraints were so damn tight. He hit the button, and the lock clicked on the metal bars. He swung the door open and jogged into her.

"Oh, my God! What... did you... do?" Her breath was shallow and quick.

Reaper looked back. The man's body twitched in death. "My job."

She turned her swollen and bruised face toward him as he rushed to remove her from the shackles. "Roman, go, leave me. Run." He glanced up to see her eyes roll and her head loll.

"Annex? Can you hear me?"

"Sometimes. Don't move, you're clear now," Anubis answered.

"Send Thirteen onto the boat. Bring in the Mercy Team. Seven women who need immediate assistance." He flicked the first restraint off her wrist and held her against the cross.

"Status on Ms. Flinn?"

"Alive. She's been beaten and is passed out." *Probably because she witnessed me decapitating that son of a bitch.* He unstrapped her other wrist.

"I copy. Mission complete?"

"Affirmative."

"Did she witness the act?"

"Yeah." He grunted his reply while he held her up, unfastening the restraints. He had no idea how bad she'd been injured, and head injuries were tricky.

"It may take time for her to come to terms with it.

I'm speaking from experience." Anubis tried to offer a bit of hope.

Reaper didn't need it. Those words were the same ones she'd said to him the day he'd killed Bert Graham. She told him to run. The woman was stronger than anyone could imagine. This time, he didn't need to run. They'd work through the fallout together.

CHAPTER 20

"**R**eaper!"

He turned his head and bellowed, "Stairs at the end of the hall." Carefully, he laid Harmony out on the steel floor, slowly placing her on the ground, watchful of her head and neck. He also made sure he was far enough away from Talib that the blood that was now oozing from the man's body wouldn't reach her.

Phoenix raced down the stairs. "Is she all right?"

"She's got a head injury. I'm not going to move her again. What's the ETA on the Mercy Team?"

"They should be here any minute." Phoenix bent down. "I didn't see him, Reaper. I didn't know, but when the watchers pulled away, it flipped a switch in my gut. I knew something was off."

Reaper pulled his eyes from Harmony to meet his friend's worried gaze. "You did everything right. By the numbers. This isn't on you. There are six women upstairs."

Phoenix blinked and looked back up the stairs. "Where?"

"You'll see two buttons spaced about ten feet apart. Push the upper button. It lifts the metal door. The one I saw was in bad shape. Get the doors open for the Mercy Team. I'll stay with Harmony."

"On it." Phoenix was gone the next second.

Reaper pushed the hair back from Harmony's face. The bone of her nose had shifted. His hand shook as he carefully examined her. A broken nose, and her cheek and eye were so swollen she wouldn't be able to open it. There was a deep laceration slicing through her lip. Blood had clotted, making the jagged split wider than it needed to be. He sat down on his butt beside her and picked up her hand. The livid purple bruising on her wrists worried him, too. She used her hands to create such beauty. If that bastard took that joy from her by binding her too tight, he *would* hunt the bastard down in hell.

He heard the muffled sound of voices through the door that Phoenix must have propped open at the top of the stairs. There was also a distant sound of sirens. "Annex, we have locals inbound."

"Ambulances only. They won't run lights and sirens until they are out of the area. Government-to-government cooperation. Once you're out, lock the vault and let the fucker decay in his own tomb," Anubis hissed. "Mercy Team is sending info on the women above."

Reaper could only imagine the horror the women above went through. He softly massaged Harmony's right wrist, praying there wasn't any permanent damage. He heard a soft footfall on the stairs.

"Incoming. Mercy Team," the woman's voice called out.

"One down." Reaper watched as the tall strawberry blonde woman emerged from the stairway.

Dressed in black and carrying a medical backpack, she froze about a foot in, glancing at the headless body. She cracked her neck and shook it off. "Nothing I can do for that one."

"Here." Reaper's voice must have pulled her from the macabre sight.

"All right. Stand clear and give me some room." The woman trotted over and started to work on Harmony. "Was she ever conscious?"

"Yes, she talked and then she passed out."

The woman nodded and continued her exam. "She's got a strong pulse; I'm concerned about the head trauma. If she comes to, keep her still. We'll get a backboard and a stretcher down here ASAP. Stay with her? She's in better shape than some of the ones upstairs."

"I won't leave her." Reaper said the words to Harmony, not the woman.

"Poet! I need your help up here," a disembodied voice called down the stairs.

"Coming!" The woman was up instantly. "Call out if you need something before we get back down here."

"She's all I need." He said the words to Harmony as he listened to the pounding of feet up above. He took her wrist in his hand again and held it, stroking the back of her hand with his thumb. "What do you think it will be like living together?" He huffed a small laugh. "You'll have time alone, but I think we could manage it." He stared down at her and sighed. "I don't have a house in the States. But nothing says we need to live there. We could live here, in Versailles. It's quieter, close to Paris and the art scene."

He heard someone at the steps and looked up.

Phoenix was there, and behind him, a tall blonde man with a reddish-blonde beard. "Doctor Maliki— Well shit, he's deader than dead."

"She's not." Phoenix cuffed the doctor on his arm.

"Right. Doctor Maliki Blue. Poet said she had a head injury. We're going to strap her up tight so the ride to the hospital won't jiggle her too much." He spoke as he worked and then directed both Reaper and Phoenix to help as he worked on Harmony. As soon as they had her on the backboard, they maneuvered the stretcher under her. The doctor had her strapped in within minutes.

"Done that a few times?" Phoenix asked as he lifted one end of the stretcher and Reaper lifted the other.

The doctor spoke from behind him. "A couple or so. The Annex will let you know which hospital she'll be taken to. It won't be the same one as the others upstairs. I understand she's family; we'll make sure she receives the best private care possible."

Reaper glanced at the holding cages that were open and empty, thank God. They paused inside the boat. The doc stepped out and then came back in. "Contact Guardian. There are people milling around. Under the streetlights, they'll see your shirt that is covered in blood." The doctor took off his lightweight black jacket and pulled his cell out before he handed it over to Reaper. "It will be tight, but at least you won't be a spectacle." He handed Reaper his ball cap. Reaper nodded, and he and Phoenix placed the stretcher on the floor. "Poet and I will take her." The doctor leaned out the door and whistled sharply. "She hates it when I do that, by the way." The man crouched down and stared at Harmony. "In the better lighting, I can see we need to get a plastic surgeon on standby. Her nose, the lip, and x-rays are going to tell the rest."

The tall strawberry blonde woman trotted into the confines of the ship. "Lassie reporting as ordered."

"Sorry, we need to haul her out of here. Give this guy your hat, please." Poet snatched her ballcap off and handed it to Phoenix. The doctor took the head of the stretcher and the woman her feet. "On three. One, two, and three." They lifted Harmony, and Reaper watched as they walked out of the ship.

"What's next?" Phoenix asked.

"We seal the doors and let him rot."

"Guardian will handle the rest?"

"As always." Reaper put the jacket and ball cap on. He waited for Phoenix to cover his red hair, and they both exited. Reaper found the panel with the keypad.

He entered random numbers until the door locked, a known failsafe of the device. Phoenix handed Reaper his weapon while blocking any view with his back. Reaper flipped it and brought the butt end down on the control panel. The thing shattered. *Good luck opening this crypt.*

"I'll need a ride."

"Lucky I have one." They both headed off the gangplank and walked directly to the car Phoenix had driven to the port. Once they were in the car and had confirmed they weren't being followed, Reaper called in.

"Annex, Fourteen and Fifteen are clear."

"Affirm. Sending directions to the hospital to Fifteen's phone. Thirteen and Seventeen are clear without incident. Fifteen, follow procedures after you drop off Fourteen. We'll contact you for Go/No Go evaluation dates and times. Fourteen, when you're clear and your woman is safe, we'll set up the Go/No Go evaluation."

"Copy," Reaper said and Phoenix nodded.

They drove through mostly deserted streets without much discussion. Phoenix pulled over a block from the hospital and took off his coat and shirt. "Wear this." He handed the shirt to Reaper, who stripped and pulled on the shirt Phoenix gave him.

"Thanks. For everything." Reaper clamped a hand on Phoenix's arm when the man turned away. "You were not at fault. Don't carry that weight."

"I get it." Phoenix shrugged. "Now I need to internalize it."

"Go back and drink some bourbon. You're not to blame. And believe me, I'd let you know if you were." Reaper winked when his friend chuffed out a small laugh. "Whatever it takes, brother."

"As long as it takes." Phoenix waved as he pulled away from the curb.

Reaper turned and jogged to the hospital. Harmony needed him to be there when she woke up to answer questions and be her advocate. To be hers. It was all he'd ever wanted, and that bastard Talib had threatened that dream. Coded or not, the man would have died tonight. He slowed to a walk and checked his appearance as best he could.

Time to reenter civilized society.

Phoenix's phone vibrated in his pocket. He pulled it out and frowned. Why was Guardian making contact again? He pulled over to the side of the road, worried that something had gone wrong at the hospital.

"Operative Fifteen."

"This is Operator Two-Seven-Four."

Phoenix put the car into park. "Did I lose you?"

"No. Can you tell me how Ms. Flinn is?"

"Excuse me?" Phoenix pulled the phone from his ear and looked at the link. It was a secure transmission.

"I was supposed to be monitoring her. I didn't react to the muffled sounds. If I had, I would have been able to call you in sooner. Please, tell me, is she okay?"

Phoenix blinked at the taillights of the cars that passed him. The ever-cool, never-ruffled operator sounded upset. "Ah, she's been roughed up pretty bad, but she's going to live."

"I should have done better." The woman's voice was almost a whisper.

Phoenix shook his head. "This wasn't your fault. You couldn't have known what was going on. Don't take this weight onto your shoulders." He smiled and slid the nugget of wisdom Reaper had laid on him to the operator.

"Ah… thank you. It is against policy for me to

reach out, but I wouldn't be able to sleep today unless I knew."

"Your supervisor is going to be upset?" Phoenix would make some calls.

"No, I'm autonomous."

"Yeah, but are you AI?" Phoenix laughed at the woman's chuckle.

"Not even a little bit. Totally human."

"Then how do you sound the exact same, year after year, and always answer the phone?"

"A trick of the trade. Autonomous, anonymous, and omnipotent... to a point."

"Sounds like fun. How'd you like to go out for coffee sometime?"

She laughed. "That is most definitely against policy."

Phoenix countered, "But you broke policy once, and you're autonomous, right?"

"And one hundred percent accountable for my actions." He could hear the smile in her voice.

"Understood. So, if I would call in just to check on how you were doing, would that be acceptable?"

There was silence on the other end. "Why would you want to do that?"

"Well, here's the thing. I'm solo, you know that. Sounds like you are, too. What would be the problem if we checked in on each other from time to time?"

"Calls are stored for evaluation. I'd have to request permission."

"From whom?"

She belted out a hardy laugh, "Oh, no, sir, that is far above your pay grade."

"Ask. I'll call you tomorrow."

"I'll ask, but…" She sounded defeated.

"I'll call tomorrow. You should have an answer, right?"

"That is correct, Sunset Operative Fifteen." She chuckled again.

"Perfect. Good night, Two-Seven-Four."

"Good night. Operator Two-Seven-Four is clear."

Phoenix pulled the phone away from his ear and shook his head. He felt like a teenager asking a girl out for the first time. A smile split his lips. Autonomous, anonymous, and semi-omnipotent with a healthy helping of accountability. That sounded like his type of woman because that description fit each Shadow to a T. What were the chances?

CHAPTER 21

Harmony woke slowly, like a radio channel fading in and out of reception. She heard voices and saw glimpses of light. Voices, light, voices, and... Her eye opened before awareness of her surroundings came into focus. She tried to turn her head. *Oh, hell. Mistake.*

"Harmony?" Roman's face appeared over her. "Hey, there you are." He smiled.

God, he looked like hell. Black circles under his eyes, and he had almost a full beard. She peeled her dry tongue off the top of her mouth. "What happened?"

The smile faded and he reached up, fingering her hair back from her face. "Talib."

Talib. *Oh, God.* Her stomach rolled and her gut clenched. An iron bar constricted across her chest and started to squeeze. Talib. She fought back nausea. He'd hurt her, hitting one side of her face again and again.

"He's gone. He'll never hurt you again." Roman didn't look at her. His thumb ran up and down her arm where he was holding on to her.

No, he wasn't *gone*. He was *dead*. She saw Roman kill him. "Why did you kill him?"

Roman lifted his eyes to her. "I had to stop him. I don't know if we'll ever know the entirety of the atrocities that he committed, but what we do know was enough to seal his fate."

The monitor tracing her heartbeat sped up as fear invaded her body like a lightning bolt—immediate, explosive, and incendiary. "You have to leave." He jerked as if she'd hit him. She grabbed at his arm although her hand didn't seem to want to work right. "The police, you have to leave. Please."

He blinked and then smiled slowly. "Harmony, I'm the good guy in this. I work for Guardian Security. What you saw me do was in the line of duty. No one will come looking for me."

She swallowed hard, wanting to believe his words. "No one?"

"I promise." He lifted her hand and kissed the back of it.

Moving even that small amount hurt. She winced, which caused her face to flame in pain, and he immediately lowered her hand. "How bad?" Roman stared at her as if debating what to tell her. "Tell me. Please."

"They reset your nose that Talib broke. The plastic surgeon did some fancy stitching on your lips, there shouldn't be a scar. You have a pretty severe concussion and a lot of soft tissue damage that will heal, and the swelling will subside. Your eye should be fine. The doc didn't see any damage, but it's swollen shut now so they want to do vision tests when the swelling subsides." He sighed and dropped his eyes to where their hands were clasped.

"What else?" She winced. "Damn it, I hurt."

"About that. They aren't giving you much to help with the pain because they're afraid it will have an effect on the baby."

"What baby?" Confusion ripped through her.

"You're pregnant. It is still very early, and the trauma you've been through has them worried, but the blood tests were conclusive."

"I…" She slid her hand to her stomach. "I used birth control." She had—most of the time. There were days when she'd missed because she was so focused on the damn paintings. "I might have forgotten to take my pill a couple times. I'm sorry."

"I'm not." Roman placed his hand on her flat stomach. "I'm not, babe. Please, tell me you want her."

"Her?"

He shrugged. "Him or her, I don't care as long as you want us."

"Want you?" A tear blurred her vision. "I love you. I want you, and God, yes, I want our baby." It was the dream she was afraid to voice for fear it would be ripped from her. Life and a family with Roman.

"Even after you saw…"

He didn't finish the statement, but she knew without a doubt what he meant. "I've known what you were capable of for the last ten years. But I knew then, and I know now, that you aren't evil. What you did then was self-defense. Bert was going to kill you. He would have if you hadn't defended yourself. The town would have convicted and locked you away for the rest of your life. Talib was evil. He… He told me when he was hitting me what he was going to do to me. He was going to kill me. Eventually."

"He had six other women. We got them all out." Roman's thumb swept away the tear that pushed over her eyelash. "You don't need to worry about him ever again."

She nodded and drew a shaky breath. "What about Bernard?"

"He was arrested by the French authorities and jailed for smuggling your work out of the country. According to Guardian, that was why your paintings were commissioned by Talib. To pay off LaVette for a debt he was owed. Bernard didn't want money; he wanted the paintings he could never own. They used the paintings as a front to conduct business. He won't see the light of day for years."

She closed her eye momentarily. "That's good. So, it's over?" She whispered the question.

"No."

She winced, opening her eye and finding him. "What?"

"We have two pieces of unfinished business. First, you have to marry me, and second, we need to buy a house. Anywhere in the world, wherever you want to live and raise a family."

The smile that tugged at her lips hurt but she smiled anyway. "I'll marry you. Can the house wait until I get out of here?"

Roman leaned forward and kissed the corner of her mouth on the side Talib hadn't injured. "Yes. Go back to sleep, my love. We'll get married tomorrow. I'll bring the officiant here."

The smile hurt, but not enough to stop. "We can wait."

"No, we can't. We've waited long enough. Go to sleep, my love. I'm here and you're safe."

Her eyelid dropped, and she hummed her agreement and slipped into an exhausted sleep.

Roman walked up behind his wife and dropped his arms over her shoulders, placing his hands on her baby bump.

She leaned back into him and sighed, "It's beautiful, isn't it?"

"You're beautiful." He bent down and kissed the top of her head.

She twisted and looked up at him. "I was talking about the mountains." She rolled her eyes. The bruising and swelling gone, she held little physical evidence of Talib's vicious attack. He dropped a kiss on her lips. "The Black Hills are okay. You're beautiful."

"I'll beg to differ. Maggie should be here in a couple hours."

"Her flight lands in an hour and a half. She has to get her bags and then the rental car, plus drive time. Your estimate is way too early."

"I wish she would have let us pick her up at the airport."

"Maggie? That woman wouldn't let anyone do anything for her."

"So, you don't think she'll move here? The mother-in-law cottage would be perfect for her."

"She's not ready to retire," he chuckled. The feisty old woman was going to be a pain in the Grahams' side as long as she could be, but he was happy Maggie was finally coming out to see them. They had purchased a beautiful log home in Spearfish Canyon, about five miles from the town of Spearfish, South Dakota. The small town had everything they wanted. The boon was he was close to the Annex and could fly in and out of the facility the majority of the time. He'd be home more than gone, and once Harmony got close to her due date, he'd been told he would be given ample time off. It was a win-win in his book.

"Should I bake something?" She turned in his arms. "I want her to fall in love with the place. She's the only family we have. I'd love for her to be closer, to help with the baby and be the grandma he won't have."

"He?" Roman chuckled.

She swatted him. "Or she. It doesn't matter as long as he or she has ten fingers and toes and is healthy." She wrapped her arms around his neck. "You know the best thing about being pregnant?"

He lifted his eyebrows, knowing exactly what she was going to say, but he tried to hold the smile from his face as he asked, "No, what?"

"It makes me horny."

He laughed and swept her off her feet. "Your wish is my command." Her laughter trailed them down the hallway to the master suite. He laid her on the bed and carefully moved to lay down beside her.

Making love to his wife now that she was pregnant had terrified him. Irrational, but true, nonetheless. He'd talked to the doctors and knew it was perfectly safe. And with his wife's propensity for frequent sex, he'd learned how to let go of the fear. Yet he was careful, so damn careful.

He worked her sundress off with tender kisses trailing over her swollen belly. His hands worshiped her body as his lips tasted and teased. His clothes came off just as slowly. There was no rush; in fact, he wouldn't be rushed. Spooning her, he lifted her top leg toward her belly and entered her, rocking back and forth slowly until he was seated.

He teased the hard nipples of her breasts with his thumbs as he kissed her. Sideways and sloppy, the need between them only intensified with the dance of their tongues. She pushed back and grabbed his hip, digging her nails into his skin, demanding more than the languid pace he'd set.

He snapped his hips forward a bit stronger but not faster. The slow burn of need trickled down his spine. Harmony's small sounds and breathless words turned the burn into an inferno. She shifted, moving away from his chest, changing the angle of his cock inside her. Her long, satisfied moan just about undid him. He held her hip and waited as her climax built. When she convulsed around him, he chased his own release. He stilled as he came inside her, his breath locked in his lungs until he'd finished.

He pulled her back into his chest. She laid on his arm and sighed, "Just a little nap."

A smile spread as he held his family. Nothing could be more perfect.

Just as he was about to doze, he heard his cell phone vibrate. He turned and glanced at the floor where his jeans laid. Careful not to wake her, he lifted her head and pulled his arm from under her head, moving a pillow in to take his place. He rolled away and reached for the jeans. He pulled the phone out to answer but didn't get that far.

"This is a recorded message from Operator Two-Seven-Four. Armageddon Protocol. Repeat, Armageddon Protocol. Heaven is under siege. Emergency recall of all operatives. Rerouting all comms through the Rose. May God bless us all."

The message began again. He stood and stared at the device in his hand.

"Roman? What's going on?"

He glanced back at the woman he loved. He sat down and told her what the recording meant.

Her eyes widened, and she gasped, "My God. Someone has declared war on Guardian."

The Beginning of the Siege

Click here to preorder:
The Siege, Book One
The Siege, Book Two

Novella

Montana Guardian: A Kings of Guardian Novella

Guardian Defenders Series

Gabriel

Maliki

John

Jeremiah

Guardian Security Shadow World

Anubis (Guardian Shadow World Book 1)

Asp (Guardian Shadow World Book 2)

Lycos (Guardian Shadow World Book 3)

Thanatos (Guardian Shadow World Book 4)

Tempest (Guardian Shadow World Book 5)

Smoke (Guardian Shadow World Book 6)

Reaper (Guardian Shadow World Book 7)

Hope City

Hope City - Brock

HOPE CITY - Brody- Book 3

Hope City - Ryker - Book 5

Hope City - Killian - Book 8

Hope City - Blayze - Book 10

STAND ALONE NOVELS

SEAL Forever - Silver SEALs

A Heart's Desire - Stand Alone

Hot SEAL, Single Malt (SEALs in Paradise)

Hot SEAL, Savannah Nights (SEALs in Paradise)

Hot SEAL, Silent Knight (SEALs in Paradise)

ABOUT THE AUTHOR

USA Today and Amazon Bestselling Author, Kris Michaels is the alter ego of a happily married wife and mother. She writes romance, usually with characters from military and law enforcement backgrounds.

Made in the USA
Coppell, TX
07 December 2021

67337213R00164